LOTERÍA

ILLUSTRATIONS BY
DANA SANMAR

LOTERÍA

KARLA ARENAS VALENTI

ALFRED A. KNOPF
NEW YORK

THIS IS A BORZOI BOOK PUBLISHED BY ALFRED A. KNOPF

Text copyright © 2021 by Karla Valenti
Jacket art and interior illustrations copyright © 2021 by Dana Sanmar

Visit us on the Web! rhcbooks.com

Educators and librarians, for a variety of teaching tools, visit us at RHTeachersLibrarians.com

Library of Congress Cataloging-in-Publication Data
Names: Valenti, Karla, author. | Sanmar, Dana, illustrator.
Title: Lotería / Karla Valenti ; illustrations by Dana Sanmar.
Description: First edition. | New York : Alfred A. Knopf, 2021. | Audience: Ages 8–12. | Audience: Grades 4–6. | Summary: In Oaxaca City, Mexico, ancient friends Life and Death discuss free will while engaged in a game of chance, with eleven-year-old Clara as the protagonist of their theories and a pawn in their game, moving inevitably towards her ultimate fate. Includes author's notes and reader's guide.
Identifiers: LCCN 2020050961 (print) | LCCN 2020050962 (ebook) | ISBN 978-0-593-17696-2 (hardcover) | ISBN 978-0-593-17697-9 (library binding) | ISBN 978-0-593-17698-6 (ebook)
Subjects: CYAC: Fate and fatalism—Fiction. | Free will and determinism—Fiction. | Lotería (Game)—Fiction. | Adventure and adventurers—Fiction. | Magic—Fiction. | Oaxaca de Juárez (Mexico)—Fiction. | Mexico—Fiction.
Classification: LCC PZ7.1.V336 Lo 2021 (print) | LCC PZ7.1.V336 (ebook) | DDC [Fic]—dc23

The text of this book is set in 12.5-point Sabon MT Pro.
Interior design by Jen Valero

Printed in the United States of America
September 2021
10 9 8 7 6 5 4 3 2 1
First Edition

TO LA FAMILIA—YOU ARE EVERYTHING TO ME

CHAPTER 1

IN WHICH LIFE AND DEATH ARRIVE, AND A GIRL'S DESTINY HANGS IN THE BALANCE

L ife sauntered into town on a wave of heat. He looked quite dapper in his black suit and matching vest, with a crisp white shirt and the tiniest hint of red peeking out of his jacket pocket: a crimson handkerchief, monogrammed.

His tall short-brimmed hat provided little shade from the blinding white sky, and his walking stick left cracks on the dry and brittle land. The high-pitched whine of cicadas pestered him incessantly.

Life raised his walking stick. With a tap, the stick opened into an umbrella that shaded him and his companion, a skeletal figure in a bright pink dress delicately embroidered with flowers and birds. A crown of roses rested on her skull; a few petals trailed behind her, plucked by a curious draft of hot air.

"Shall we?" Life asked.

"We shall," his companion replied, brushing dust off her sleeve. She may have been Lady Death (though she preferred to go by the name Catrina), but that didn't mean she was immune to the allure of beauty.

Catrina placed her bony wrist, clinking with gilded bangles, upon Life's outstretched arm. Together, they walked up to the main plaza in front of the Santo Domingo cathedral.

"I wonder where everyone is?" Life asked.

"Taking shelter, no doubt," Catrina replied.

It was already one of the hottest mornings on record in the hottest summer anyone in Oaxaca City could remember. People burrowed deep inside their houses shaded by the massive branches of purple-flowered jacaranda trees. Exhausted fans made eddies of hot air bloated with lethargic mosquitoes and flies. The ceramic tile floors, usually so cool to the touch, radiated an infernal heat. Jugs of water steamed like pots on a stove.

Catrina's bracelets rattled against her bones as she flicked her bangled wrist, spreading out a fan. Made of black lace and glinting with tiny white pearls, the fan was a gift from one of her admirers—of whom she had plenty.

It had been left for her on one of the many marigold-covered altars that blossomed around the Día de los Muertos celebration, tucked between candied skulls and photos of lost relatives. A note attached to the gift read, "Por favor cuídalos." *Of course I'll take care of them.* Catrina watched over all her wards with a fierceness matched only by Life.

"Well, let's get to it," Life said.

"Let's," Catrina replied, and she began to fan herself. A cool breeze spread out from the black lace, a welcome relief in the searing heat. Strings of silver frost emanated from the fan, drifting out like so many wishes.

Beneath their makeshift parasol, Life and Death followed the silver strands unfurling before them.

They peeked into a doorway where a little boy played with a kitten in a box while his mother made a batch of tortillas to sell later in the day. The kitten meowed at the intruders, and the little boy looked up. He saw a handsome, well-dressed man and a beautiful woman with creamy brown skin and long dark hair.

Life nodded at the boy. Catrina smiled.

The two companions moved on.

Next they passed a peeling wall painted with a faded mermaid clutching a basket of fruit. Bold letters above the mermaid spelled the store's name: LA FRUTERÍA SIRENA. It was run by a wrinkled man who had been there longer than anyone could remember.

The man and his wrinkles were fast asleep on a hammock strung up in the middle of the fruit shop. A strategically placed fan spun endlessly beside the slumbering man, its blades in a losing battle against the heat.

Catrina took extra notice of the old man; his light was fading, and he would soon be joining her. But not today.

They walked past La Rosa hair salon and the aptly named nursery La Maceta, the Flowerpot. Meaty cacti bursting with fruit stood sentry on either side of the door. Towering palm trees shaded the owner while he read a newspaper.

At the end of the street, they approached a small church. Life gazed up at the brightly colored papel picado—paper cutouts—tied from the bell tower to the lush trees surrounding the church. Each cutout depicted a scene of love. Crushed flower petals clung to the papers and stained the ground.

"There was a wedding," Catrina said.

"May the couple live long and well," Life replied, briefly bowing his head. The couple would indeed go

on to live long and well, never knowing they owed their good fortune to the blessing of this strange visitor. But that is a story for another time.

Catrina fanned herself again, sending out a new wave of silver strands.

At that very moment, on another cobblestone street, a young girl in a small house with walls painted robin's-egg blue looked up. With an urgency she couldn't quite explain, she turned her gaze toward the window.

From her perch, the girl could just make out the twin crosses that crowned the cathedral's blue-and-white cupolas. A lone white dove beat its wings against the hot sky.

The girl rose and opened her window.

The church bells tolled.

"Clara," the girl's mother called. "Come."

A hint of cool breeze entered Clara's room. Hesitant at first, the breeze tentatively explored the confines of the space, just big enough for a child-sized bed, a two-drawer dresser, and the girl herself.

The breeze wrapped around the girl and tightly wove itself into her braids. A shiver ran down Clara's back, and she shook her head, trying to dislodge the breeze from her hair. She tugged at a stray strand of silver.

"Child, I need you," her mother called.

"I'm coming." Clara set down her sketch, a messy doodle of a horse with eagle's wings.

Clara was not a good artist, and she knew that. Perhaps with more time and resources, she could develop this interest into an actual talent. As it was, she could sketch only on weekend mornings before her parents awoke. The rest of the time she spent in school and helping her parents run their small restaurant, La Casa de Juana.

The restaurant had started off as just a few tables in their living room, where Clara's parents liked to host dinners for friends. However, as word of Juana's talents in the kitchen spread, more and more tables were added. Their guests insisted on helping cover some of the costs of the food and preparation, and the living room was gradually transformed into a restaurant.

"Clara!" her mom called.

"Okay, okay," Clara called back, and made her way to the kitchen.

Juana was Clara's mother, and by all accounts the best cook in Oaxaca. Her tamales were light and flavorful. Wrapped in banana leaves, the cornmeal patties were stuffed with mole, corn, chicken, and black beans, or pineapples and raisins, then steamed and sold still hot to the touch.

Juana also made the best tlayudas: large, thin, and partially toasted tortillas covered with a spread of beans, cheese, lettuce, and avocado, topped with beef, pork, seafood, or, Clara's favorite, mushrooms.

Juana's specialty dishes were many: tasajo, chorizo, cecina, guacamole, dozens of salsas. But what made La Casa de Juana truly special was the hot chocolate.

Clara's mother had inherited the recipe from her mother, who had in turn received it from her mother, and she from her mother . . . and so forth for generations.

At some point, Clara had taken it upon herself to sample hot chocolate from every vendor in the city, just to see if what people said was true. There was no con-

test. Her mother's combination of hand-ground cacao, almonds, cinnamon, and sugar was unmatched.

"She must have a touch of magic!" the other vendors speculated, and their words felt as true as the sharp bite of cinnamon on Clara's tongue.

Clara walked into their small kitchen to find her mother bent over a large ceramic pitcher bubbling on the stove, surrounded by a swirl of scents. A long wooden stick jutted up from the thick dark mixture. The molinillo was a wooden whisk, specially designed to yield the frothiest hot chocolate.

"Gracias, mija," Juana said. "We're meeting with your cousins later today, and I need to pick up some things for the picnic. Can you keep an eye on this while I run to the mercado?"

"Sure." Clara stepped up to the stove.

"What's that in your hair?" Juana asked.

Clara looked down at her braids and marveled at the dozens of thin silvery strands interlaced with her own dark strands of hair. She pulled at the ribbons at the ends of her braids, loosening the plaits. Her hair spilled out, releasing the silver strands. She watched them slip gently to the ground.

"Strange," Clara said, retying her hair.

But the deed was already done. She had been chosen.

Clara took the molinillo from her mother.

"I won't be long," Juana said.

"Okay."

"Do not stop stirring that," Juana added, giving Clara a stern look. "It'll burn."

As she stepped outside, Juana stumbled over a bottle at the threshold of her house, discarded the previous evening by a drunken man.

Had the bottle not been there, Juana would have noticed the pack of stray dogs sitting quietly beneath Clara's window. And she would have remarked on the unusual flowers that had suddenly sprouted along the wall of the house. And she surely would have paused at the sight of a festively clad woman on the arm of an impeccably dressed gentleman watching her from across the street. But Juana saw none of that.

Not that it would have made a difference.

"It's settled, then," Life said.

"And so it is," Catrina agreed, gathering the silver strands of frost that had, in one instant, changed Clara's fate forever.

CHAPTER 2

IN WHICH LIFE AND DEATH
BEGIN A GAME OF CHANCE

After Catrina collected all the silver strands, she and Life found a cool patch of shade in a small plaza not far from the blue house. In the center of the plaza, a stone fountain defied the heat with a cascade of bubbling water.

Gnarly trees, as ancient as Life, encircled the plaza. Their rough trunks split five, six, seven times, like fingers reaching up to the sky. Their branches interlaced in a tangle of leaves so dense no sunlight could penetrate. Birds hopped from branch to branch, calling to each other, while cicadas thrummed to the pulse of the sun.

From his jacket pocket Life pulled out his handkerchief. He unfolded it neatly, then spread it out in the air before him, where it lay perfectly flat, suspended like a magic carpet in flight. The handkerchief grew, expanding on all four sides until it was the size of a small table.

From another pocket Life extracted a single card displaying the image of a man in a suit with a top hat and a cane. "El Catrín," the card read.

Life set the card on a corner of the table and tapped it. Beneath El Catrín fifty-three cards materialized, each with a different image. He shuffled the deck of cards three times, then placed it facedown in the center of the table.

From her skirts Catrina produced a delicately embroidered bundle. She tugged at the ribbon around the bundle and pulled out a small circle of glass framed in silver. Catrina placed the glass on the table between them. In the clear oval, Clara's image materialized, a small window into the girl's life.

Next, Catrina poured out a handful of frijoles—beans as black as night—and gathered them into a pile in the center, beside the cards.

"You won last time," Life said, holding out a spread of tablas, cardboard placards with a different image printed in each of the sixteen squares.

"And the time before that," Catrina replied, selecting one of the tablas.

"I do hope this isn't becoming a trend," Life added, choosing his own tabla.

"I suppose we'll have to see." Catrina smiled.

The two laid out their tablas on the handkerchief table and placed a handful of black beans beside them.

"Let the game begin," Life said.

La Lotería was a simple game of chance. The first

player to get four cards in a straight line—horizontal, vertical, or diagonal—would win. A win by Catrina would deliver Clara into her hands. A win by Life would spare the child, granting Clara a long life.

And so it was that the fate of a child tending to a pot of hot chocolate hung on a pile of beans and a deck of cards.

The players had three days to complete the game and deliver their prize, after which they would part ways for another year, meeting only to play another round. The rules were clear: if they failed to complete their game in the allotted time, it would be their final round, and they would never meet again. Those thirty-six hours were a rare gift, and one the friends cherished deeply.

Catrina pinched a black bean in her knobby fingers.

Life flipped over the first card. "EL QUE LE CANTÓ A SAN PEDRO NO LE VOLVERÁ A CANTAR," he said.

"THE ONE THAT SANG FOR ST. PETER WILL NEVER SING FOR HIM AGAIN." Catrina repeated the riddle as the two friends studied their tablas. "The rooster."

"That it is," Life replied, discarding the card in the center of the table.

"Alas, no rooster for me," Catrina said.

"Or me."

Life drew a second card. "EL QUE A BUEN ÁRBOL SE ARRIMA BUENA SOMBRA LE COBIJA."

Catrina laughed, pointing at the branches overhead. "How fitting! HE WHO APPROACHES A GOOD TREE IS BLANKETED BY GOOD SHADE."

She placed a black bean on the image of a tree on her tabla. "And so it begins!"

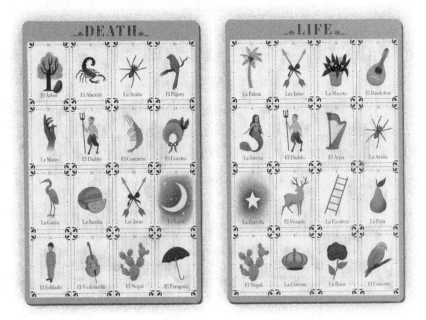

CHAPTER 3

IN WHICH A FAILURE LEADS TO UNEXPECTED CONSEQUENCES

In the blue house, Clara looked up from the chocolate she was diligently stirring. A sudden and invisible weight pressed upon her shoulders. The chocolate became impossibly thick, and she strained to move the molinillo. Just as quickly, the feeling vanished, and the molinillo flew out of her hand, splattering chocolate all over the wall.

As Clara reached for a cloth to clean up the mess, she could not shake the feeling that something important had just transpired.

A noise in the restaurant interrupted her thoughts.

"Hello?" she called out. "Papi?"

She listened closely, but all she could hear was the bubbling mix on the stove.

"Is anyone there?" Clara stepped through the beads that separated the kitchen from the dining room.

Six square tables were draped in plastic tablecloths, with salsas for centerpieces. An old radio tucked behind the counter burst into a lively canción norteña. Clara jumped.

"Sorry, mi hija," her father said, appearing behind the counter. "I didn't mean to startle you. This old box was giving me a hard time." He walked over to an even older TV bolted to a shelf in the corner. The black-and-white image on the screen showed her father's favorite luchador, El Apache, locked in the grip of another beefy wrestler.

Clara's father picked up a broom. Stealing glances at the match, he danced from table to table with the broom in his hand. When he swept past Clara, he grabbed her by the arm and pulled her into his dance.

"¡Buenos días!" he sang, his voice deep, steady, and rich.

"Good morning," Clara replied. "Everything okay?"

"I think so." As her father spun her around, Clara took in the restaurant her parents had opened when she was no more than a year old. It was here that she had learned to eat and speak and walk and dance. It was here that she had learned to play dominoes and viuda negra, the card game favored by all the local widows. It was in this very spot that she had experienced her first artistic inspiration after seeing the distorted reflection of a cicada that had flown into a drinking glass.

The walls were painted with colorful scenes, as vibrant now as they had been ten years ago. On the wall behind the counter, cool blue waves shimmered, tipped with glimmers of gold sun. A fishing boat bobbed in the distance, the men's heads bent toward each other in a never-ending conversation. Beyond them, a small island glittered: La Isla de las Ranas, named for all the frogs meticulously drawn on the beach.

Another wall looked like a seafood stand at the market: there was a purple octopus tentacle and a rubbery squid, pink shrimp, and mounds of white scallops. On the opposite wall, a fruit stand boasted towers of orange papayas, spiky pineapples, prickly pears, and magueys. There were melons, bananas, and bright green kiwis. Customers said the artwork alone made their mouths water.

Her father grunted and stopped mid-dance.

"Papi? Are you okay?"

He pulled out a chair and sat down, groaning. "My back," he said. "It's as rickety as that old radio." He winked at Clara. "I just need a moment to rest."

"Here, let me finish for you." Clara took the broom from him and began sweeping.

She hadn't gotten far when her father said, "What's that smell?"

Clara gasped, dropped the broom, and raced back through the beads into the kitchen. The chocolate mix was violently sputtering all over the stove. Curls of black smoke filled the kitchen. She grabbed the molinillo and stirred, but she could already tell the mixture was ruined, the liquid clotted and sticking to the bottom of the pan.

"Ugh!" She lifted the heavy pitcher off the burner.

"What happened?" her father called from the dining room.

"I burned the hot chocolate," Clara called back. "Again." She sighed.

"Do you need help?"

"No, Papi. But thanks."

Clara dumped the ruined chocolate and wiped her hands on a towel. She reached for a small metal tin resting on a shelf next to the stove and pulled out a faded yellow piece of paper. The edges were ragged, and a triangle was missing at the top where it had been folded and the crease had eventually become a tear. This was the famous hot chocolate recipe, written in Abuelita Esperanza's impeccable penmanship.

Clara read each step twice before meticulously following the instructions, word for word. By the time Juana returned, a new pot of chocolate was bubbling on the stove. It wasn't even a good approximation of the chocolate her mother made, but Clara knew her mom would easily remedy that.

"It just needs a bit of salt," Juana said, tasting the new batch and adding some salt. "And perhaps a bit more . . ."

This and that were added, then a pinch of something else.

"See?" Juana concluded. "You did a great job."

The result of Juana's magic touch was a decadent pot of rich and creamy goodness.

Later that afternoon at the family picnic, Juana would tell everyone that Clara had made the hot chocolate. They all complimented her, and when she tried to explain that it was her mother behind the magic, they refused to believe her.

Clara knew they were being kind—that was what family did—but it still made her feel good. And it was this very feeling of ease and self-assurance that ultimately prompted her to agree to a seemingly small request, with unexpected consequences.

CHAPTER 4

IN WHICH A DRAGON
IS DEVOURED

Clara's cousins had long been searching for the entrance to the Gruta de Oro. They knew that the Golden Grotto, with its solid gold stalagmites and stalactites, was just a myth. But they were no strangers to mysteries-come-true, and so, after the lively picnic lunch, they set off in search of gold.

The cousins took turns listening for whispers in the trees.

"There!"

"No, that way!"

"It's my turn to lead!"

Through fields of tall grass dotted with flowers and over clear streams speckled with stones, they followed their instincts to a cavern hidden behind a dense curtain of vines and shrubbery.

Behind the vines, and inside the grotto, enormous pillars of wet sediment rose from the ground to a ceiling out of sight. A trick of light tinged them gold. Not exactly the Gruta de Oro, but close enough.

Massive stalactites clung to the ceiling. Drips of water traveled down the solidified cones of mineral, gathering at an impossibly sharp point before plunging to meet the equally sharp stalagmites below.

Over the years the droplets had created ghoulish formations, like monsters slowly melting. Their cries of agony seemed to echo through the cavern as the wind raced to find the exit.

"Whoa!" whispered Esteban, Clara's youngest cousin. "It *is* real. . . ."

"Come on—let's check it out," said his oldest brother, Manolo.

"I'm not so sure about this." Clara gripped Esteban's hand tightly.

"But think of all the gold!" Esteban said.

"It looks pretty slippery," she replied. "And besides, I don't think it's really gold."

"We'll be careful." Esteban urged her on. "Come on. You promised you would go with me."

The yawning darkness dripped with cold: an accident just waiting to happen.

"*Pleeeaaase*," Esteban said. "I know you're nervous. But you can do it."

Clara frowned. "Of course I can do it. I'm just worried about . . . about you."

Esteban grinned. "Don't worry about me! As long as we're together, we'll be fine."

"Are you coming?" Manolo called out. "Riches await!"

The older boys began moving deeper into the cave.

Esteban waited for Clara, one foot poised at the entrance.

Clara sighed. "Fine." She adjusted the bag slung across her chest. "But we need to be really careful."

"We will." Esteban nodded very solemnly.

The ground was slick and uneven, with murky pools of water every few steps. Esteban's four brothers, Manolo, Victor, Ricardo, and Antonio, moved deftly through the towers of calcified stone, chattering excitedly.

"Do you think we should take a piece home?" Victor asked. His hand was wrapped around a stalagmite, glimmering gold in a slanting beam of sun that had managed to cut through the vines over the entrance. "A bit of gold would go a long way."

Clara's family lived meagerly, but they made ends meet with their small restaurant. For Esteban's family, on the other hand, getting by was a daily struggle. Their father had died a few years earlier, leaving Esteban's mother a poor widow with five boys, now aged fourteen, thirteen, eleven, ten, and eight.

"No!" Manolo called out. "You'll curse us. Remember what the legend says!"

"The legend's not true," Victor replied. "And anyway, this isn't *real* gold." Still, he moved his hand away.

"Maybe there's other treasure," Esteban said. "Real treasure."

"Clever little brother!"

The next sound Clara heard was a rapid clicking from Ricardo as the boys walked deeper into the cave.

Echolocation is not a skill that most children have, but Esteban and each of his brothers had been born with unique talents. Indeed, all of Clara's family had what she called "hueli": abilities that, while not earth-shattering, were definitely remarkable and gave each of them a certain special quality that Clara felt she sorely lacked.

Manolo excelled at woodworking, and had inherited their father's carpentry business. Victor was a master of prestidigitation, or sleight of hand. He was often hired as a magician for children's parties, and no matter how closely people watched, they could never quite figure out his tricks.

Ricardo was an echolocator, and Antonio was a brilliant student—a genius, some said. Esteban's talent was a frighteningly accurate gut instinct that bordered on fortune-telling. Their mother, Chita, was a healer, and people traveled great distances to consult with her.

Even Clara's father and mother were gifted: one as a musician, the other as a cook.

But the gifts stopped there.

For some reason Clara could never understand, she did not possess a single talent. She was extraordinarily ordinary. In fact, she could not carry a tune, or make a meal to save her life. She had tried gardening but killed everything she planted. She had attempted to care for a stray cat, but the cat left less than a day later. She couldn't even play a decent game of soccer. If anything, she had an uncanny ability to make mistakes.

"Listen!" Ricardo said.

The children stopped in their tracks. Wind whistled past towers of stone, carrying with it a hundred echoing drips. And something else.

No me olvides, amor. . . .

Clara could vaguely pick out the words.

Nunca estoy lejos de ti.
Tu vida ha sido un dulzor,
Un regalo para mí.

Do not forget me, my love.
I am never far from you.
Your life has been a sweetness,
A gift for me.

"Where is that coming from?" one of the boys asked.

"It sounds like it's coming from there!" Manolo pointed toward the darkness of the cavern looming ahead.

"But that's Mami's voice," Esteban said, and he was right. It was his mother's voice—a strange acoustic effect of the particular structure of the cave—accompanied by the faint notes of a guitar. The singing faded, swallowed up by the darkness. But let us not forget their singing, for it will yet play a role in this story.

The older boys laughed and resumed their exploration, their voices echoing wildly in the vast space.

"They're leaving," Esteban said.

"Wait up!" Clara called out, but the brothers ignored her.

Clara tightened her grip on Esteban's hand, and they stepped from stone to stone. It was slow progress, and soon the older boys were far ahead and out of sight.

"Where did they go?" Esteban asked.

"I don't know," Clara replied, peering into the wet darkness.

Esteban groaned. "They always leave me behind!" He turned to Clara. "What should we do?"

Ricardo's clicks and snippets of the boys' conversation ricocheted off the walls. But she couldn't tell where the sounds were actually coming from.

Her heart sped up as she recognized the familiar pangs of an impossible choice. If she gave in to her fear, she would surely fail Esteban. But if they forged onward into the dark cavern, she was bound to make a mistake and fail them both.

It was an inescapable trap.

"I'm sorry," she said. "I don't think we should go on."

"Okay," Esteban sighed. He dragged his feet behind Clara as they made their way back to the cave entrance.

They found a stone cushioned by moss and warmed by the sun, a seat just big enough for the two of them to sit on while they waited for the older boys to return. Disappointment pulsed off Esteban's body.

To kill time, they watched butterflies catching sunlight on their wings; they swapped stories about silly neighbors; they made bracelets out of tall grass. When they had run out of riddles, Clara opened her bag.

Once upon a time it had been a birthday gift from her parents, containing a new sketchbook, a set of pencils, a sharpener, and an excellent eraser. Now it held the nubs of pencils, a dulled sharpener, and the worn remainder of a once excellent eraser, along with a few blank pages in her sketchbook.

"Do you want me to draw something?" she asked.

"Yes!"

"Okay, what should I draw?"

"A dragon!"

"You always want dragons." Clara laughed, but she was already taking out her sketchbook.

"With two heads," Esteban added.

"Got it." Clara drew a rough outline. She had to erase it three times before it resembled anything close to a dragon. By then, Esteban had also requested wings. "One with scales and the other with feathers. And a black tongue and a forked tale and claws like a falcon's!"

"How's this?" She held up the sketch.

Esteban studied it closely. As he always did, he pointed out small details Clara had added to the drawing: the letter *E* on one of the scales, a *C* on one of the feathers, a ring around one of the dragon's toes. "It's great! Thank you."

Clara ripped out the page and handed it to him.

"Hey!" Ricardo called from inside the cave. "Come here—check this out!"

Clara tucked her sketchbook and pencils in her bag. "Look what we found."

The boys stood just inside the entrance, and at their

feet were a dozen small, delicate ceramic bowls. Some were cracked and missing pieces; others were covered in faint patches of red paint. They all had intricate carvings of swirls and circles, spirals and dots.

"They're beautiful!" Clara said.

Esteban set down his drawing and picked up one of the bowls.

At that very moment a gust of wild wind brushed past Esteban. For many days this wind had traveled, starting at the peak of a snowcapped volcano and gradually gathering heat as it descended. Unaccustomed to the high temperature, the wind sought refuge in the cool dampness of the cave. As it blew past Esteban, it swept the drawing of the dragon along with it.

Caught up in the excitement of discovery, none of the children noticed.

The drawing traveled into the deepest depths of the cave, through a vast network of underground tunnels, finally coming to rest among a distant mass of tangled roots. Those roots, thousands of years old and voracious in their hunger, eagerly devoured the paper and the dragon upon it—an act with devastating consequences for Clara and Esteban.

CHAPTER 5

"EL ÁRBOL"

The following day and six miles away, in the town center of Santa María del Tule, an ancient tree whose roots dug deep into a tunnel quietly completed a small transformation.

With the widest trunk of any tree in the world, El Árbol del Tule was an arboreal behemoth. It had been growing for thousands of years—by some estimates, as many as six millennia—and its canopy could shelter up to five hundred people. At that moment, however, only twelve people were benefiting from its shade: a small tour group and a cluster of local children challenging each other to spot new shapes among the trunk's elaborate knots and gnarls, many of which resembled animals or mythical creatures.

The tour guide called for everyone to link arms and encircle the tree. He invited the children to join them, a futile task, with fewer than half of the thirty people required to create a full ring around the trunk. The point was made: El Árbol del Tule was massive.

It was during this exercise that one of the children made an interesting observation. On the tree's trunk, directly at his eye level, a knot of bark had twisted into a creature he had never before seen on this tree.

Born in Santa María del Tule, Esteban had grown up in the tree's shadow. He knew every nook and cranny, every twist and turn, and definitely every knot and gnarl of this giant. There was no doubt about the matter—the figure on the tree was brand-new.

However, it wasn't the newness of the shape that took him by surprise; it was what it resembled: an exact replica of the dragon Clara had sketched for him the day before.

Esteban had looked for the drawing after it was swept away, but he never found it, and Clara had promised she'd make him another one. He'd not given it another thought, until now.

The tour group moved on, following the guide toward a waiting bus. Some of the tourists handed coins to Esteban's friends (the main purpose of the children's visit to the tree that day), but Esteban lingered behind, slowly tracing the lines of the creature on the tree. There was the *E* on one of the scales, the *C* on a dragon's feather, the ring wrapped around one of its toes. He couldn't make sense of the sight before him, although he tried to convince himself that there was a perfectly good explanation for it.

In a rush of giggles, the other children raced back to Esteban to combine their newly acquired loot and split it evenly. Esteban barely registered the handful of coins he was given.

A dozen more tour groups would arrive that day, making the children's pockets bulge with clinking metal. Under ordinary circumstances, Esteban would have been delighted with his bounty. But as he emptied his coins into a small jar by his bed that evening, his mother noticed his sullen mood.

"Are you hungry?" Chita asked. "There's some pan amarillo and requesón in the kitchen." The yellow bread made with egg yolk and sugar was Esteban's favorite, and normally he loved the stringy cheese. However, it all tasted bland and insipid as he struggled to come up with an explanation for what he'd seen.

Of course, he had to consider the possibility that the creature had always been on the tree and he had never noticed it before. But the other children had also spotted the creature, and they all agreed it was new. No, this was definitely a recent addition.

The situation was giving him a headache, and a growing sense of unease.

"Esteban? Are you okay?" his mother asked.

"I'm fine, Mami. I'm just thinking about something."

"Can I help?"

"I'm not sure. . . ." He hesitated. "I have a feeling something bad is about to happen."

His mother frowned.

Esteban had inherited his premonitory talent from his father. People would come from all over the state to meet with Esteban's father. It was said he was never wrong, that his predictions were true to a tee. The only premonition he ever missed was the one that had mattered most.

He had been walking home from work one day when he was struck by lightning. There's a saying that lightning never strikes twice in the same spot, but Esteban knew that wasn't true. For his dad was struck in the very spot where *his* father had been struck twenty years earlier. Some people said it was destiny, that the lightning death of Esteban's father had been written in the stars. When Esteban mentioned this to Clara, she said she didn't believe in destiny.

"Things in life just happen," she said. "And that includes death."

Destiny or not, one thing was certain: after the lightning strike, Esteban began to experience premonitions of his own, and like his father, he was never wrong.

"What makes you think something bad is about to happen?" Chita asked. She was always careful to keep her alarm in check at Esteban's proclamations, but she knew better than to ignore them. "And how bad?"

"Well, I saw something today that I can't explain." He described the incident at the tree, adding, "It seems like a message. Or an omen."

His mother nodded.

"It might be a coincidence," Esteban went on, although neither of them believed in coincidences. They knew that things always happened for a reason. The reason might not be evident at first, but by the end of the journey it was always clear.

"We need to call Juana and tell her," his mother said. "She should keep a closer eye on things until the feeling goes away."

Juana was used to such portentous calls from her sister, and she put great stock in Esteban's premonitions. If Esteban thought something bad was going to happen, then something bad *was* going to happen.

"Okay," Juana said after hearing Chita's concern. "I'll talk to Clara. And perhaps we should see the tree," she added. "Just to make sure?"

The sisters agreed to meet the following day.

CHAPTER 6

IN WHICH LIFE AND DEATH
DISCUSS FREE WILL

Seated under a large tree overlooking the blue house, Catrina gazed up at the stain of lilac melting across the sky, gradually deepening into purple, then indigo. A chain of clouds drifted away to find the sun, and as they departed, they draped a canopy of stars over the city.

"Such a simple thing, the turning of the earth," Catrina said. "And yet it creates such extraordinary beauty."

"That it does," Life agreed.

When the parade of colors had faded away, Catrina turned to her companion.

"A toast?" she asked.

He nodded.

Catrina reached into her skirts and pulled out

two small black pottery bowls. A pattern of geometric shapes ran around the rim of one bowl, which she handed to Life. Roses crowned the rim of the other, which she kept for herself.

"This is quite something," Life said, admiring his bowl's smooth sheen and elaborate design.

"It's from this area," she replied. "A gift from an admirer."

Life smiled. Catrina was as competitive in her personal life as she was in play, and she never missed an opportunity to let Life know exactly how beloved she was.

Extending his finger, Life touched the soil at his feet. Instantly, a jet of clear water flowed upward. He filled Catrina's bowl first. Moonlight glanced off the water in the black receptacle as he passed it to her. He then filled his own bowl.

As quickly as the jet of water arose, it vanished.

"To the first day!" Life said.

Catrina tapped the deck of cards on their makeshift table. "To the inevitable."

"Oh?"

"Well, the cards are shuffled; their order is already defined," Catrina said. "Which is to say, the winner of the game is a foregone conclusion. We play only to reveal the inevitable."

"In that case, to the winner!" Life said.

Catrina nodded and cupped her bowl delicately, bringing it up to her skeletal jaw and letting the clear liquid drip down a phantom throat.

Life followed suit, then set down his moonlit bowl. He picked up the top card from the deck before him.

"EL QUE CON LA COLA PICA, LE DAN UNA PALIZA," he called out. "HE WHO STINGS WITH HIS TAIL WILL GET A BEATING."

"The scorpion!" Catrina placed a black bean on her tabla.

At their feet a dirt-colored scorpion with a small black dot on its back scurried away, carrying its stinger toward certain destiny.

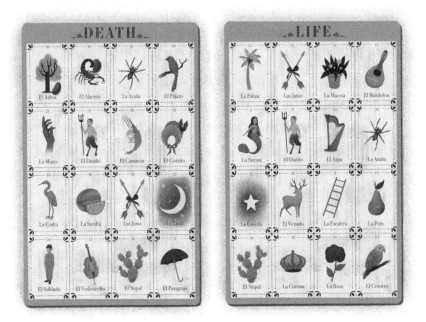

CHAPTER 7

"EL ALACRÁN"

The family agreed that Clara's father would stay behind to run the restaurant while Clara and her mother went to Santa María del Tule. Thus, on the evening prior to their departure, Clara and Juana worked late into the night getting the food ready for the following day.

"Remember, don't stop stirring." Juana pointed at the pitcher of hot chocolate simmering on the stove. She moved around the kitchen like a dancer onstage, always in graceful motion. Her hands never stopped as she chopped, sliced, rolled, fried, tasted, seasoned, tasted again.

"I can do more than this," Clara said, diligently stirring the hot chocolate.

"It's okay," Juana replied. "What you're doing is a big help."

Clara knew this was true; however, her mother needed more help than this. Despite her ease in the kitchen, it was clear Juana was distracted. Her concern had gradually electrified the room. Clara's skin tingled, and the hair on her arms stood on end.

"Mami!" Clara cried. "Careful, you're burning the food."

Juana had already ruined a batch of tamales and thrown away the first mix of hot chocolate when she added salt instead of sugar. Now black smoke rose from the comal, a flat pan in which she had been roasting peppers. She swiftly removed the peppers from the comal and, without a thought, began peeling off the charred skin.

"Ouch!" she cried as the steaming peppers burned her fingers.

"Mami!" Clara rushed over to help her mother. "You knew they were hot."

"I'm sorry. I'm just distracted." Juana ran her hands under cold water.

"You're tired," Clara said. "And I know you're worried. You should go to bed."

"No, no," Juana said. She turned off the water and returned to the stove. "I still have too much to do."

"Fine," Clara said. "Then at least take a small break." She led Juana to the hot chocolate and put the molinillo in her mother's hand. "Don't stop stirring."

This time Juana didn't resist.

"What should I work on?" Clara asked.

Juana pointed at the masa sitting in a bowl on the counter. "We need more tortillas."

"I can do that," Clara replied. She plucked bits of dough and rolled them into small balls that she flattened with a tortilla press. The tortillas were shaped unevenly and thinner than her mother's, but they would have to do.

Juana stirred the hot chocolate, and for a few minutes the two worked quietly. Then Juana's voice broke the silence. "What do you think it means?" she asked.

"What Esteban saw?" Clara asked. "Or his feeling?"

"Both."

Clara was embarrassed about the attention her sketch was receiving. She rarely showed her drawings to anyone, and now the whole family was talking about it. They'd even asked her to draw it again so they could compare it with the growth on the tree.

"I think he saw something that reminded him of my drawing," Clara said. It seemed impossible to believe that her *exact* drawing had been replicated on the tree trunk. "He has a very active imagination, you know."

Juana did not respond, but the tension in the room eased just a little. Clara finished pressing the tortillas and moved on to the now-cooled peppers. As she peeled off their charred skin, Juana spoke up again.

"And what do you make of his premonition? He's always right about those. Always."

Clara nodded and finished peeling the peppers. "I know," she sighed, reaching for a knife.

"Wait," Juana said. "I'll do that."

"Mami, I can cut peppers."

"Of course you can," Juana replied, but she still took the knife from Clara. "Why don't you start cleaning up? I'll just finish this salsa, and then we can go to bed."

The two worked side by side while the moon looked on, its strands of silver light interlacing with the glow of the kitchen fire. In this braid of silver and gold, a dirt-colored scorpion with a black dot entered the room.

The scorpion scuttled out of view, then slowly inched along the floor under the blue-and-white-tiled counter. It made its way around baskets laden with red, white, and yellow onions. It crawled through a crate of potatoes and past burlap bags heavy with rice and dried beans. Clicking softly, the scorpion circumvented a cluster of long-forgotten limes, their skins brown and hard, before it arrived at the other end of the kitchen, where it began a steady climb up the wall.

Juana reached for a jar of cumin, her fingers barely missing the scorpion rest- ing on the shelf next to the oregano. The scor- pion moved on, past an assortment of ceramic bowls of different sizes, past the bundles of dried  herbs and ropes of chiles hanging to dry. And then it reached the top of the wall, where it extended a seg- mented leg and gripped the ceiling.

Clara had been busy during the scorpion's walk: food had been put away, dishes had been washed (only one bowl had broken), the floor had been swept. But now she stood still, poised directly beneath the arachnid.

She watched Juana wring her hands on her apron.

"Don't worry, Mami," Clara told her. "I'm sure we'll get some answers tomorrow."

The scorpion released its grip on the ceiling and plunged toward the girl.

"You're right," Juana said, and she pulled Clara into a hug. The movement was slight, but it was enough.

The scorpion landed on the kitchen floor inches from Clara's shoe, a precarious place for such a creature. As quickly as it could, it edged away from the looming threat of Clara's foot.

"We should get some sleep," Juana said, releasing her daughter. Clara stepped back into the now scorpion-free space.

But the dirt-colored fiend with a black dot on its back still had a role to play. Hidden behind the leg of a chair, the scorpion watched as the girl and her mother turned off the kitchen lights and said good night. The moon lingered for a while, perhaps waiting to see what would happen. Eventually, however, it withdrew in search of more interesting sights upon which to gaze.

But the scorpion, infinitely patient, settled down to wait out the night.

Miles away, Esteban tossed and turned in his sleep. A stab of pain, sudden and sharp, propelled him out of bed. He groaned, clutching his stomach as he raced to the bathroom, where he promptly deposited his supper. The sickening dread he'd felt at the tree had intensified with every passing minute.

His body smoldered as the heat brought his blood to

a boil. He splashed water on his face. Clouds of steam fogged up the window. He had experienced high fevers before, especially connected to his premonitions, but he'd never had one quite this intense.

His vision blurred as he tiptoed past his mother's room into the kitchen. With trembling hands he poured himself a glass of water, spilling its contents all over the counter and on the floor. But he didn't care. The cool, clear liquid raced down his throat, instantly quashing the heat inside him. He poured himself another glass, and then another, until, with a final fizzle, his fever vanished, the puddle on the floor the only evidence of its existence.

But even then sleep evaded the boy, who knew, without knowing how, that everything was about to change forever.

CHAPTER 8

IN WHICH CLARA
TAKES A TRIP

The following morning, Clara woke early. The sun had just begun to wash away the night sky, sending a few faint rays of gold and orange to light up her room as Clara dressed. The scent of cinnamon-laced coffee indicated her parents were already up.

In the kitchen, Clara's father cooked some scrambled eggs and frijoles while her mother packed a picnic basket for the day ahead. A pile of crispy tortillas sat on the table. They ate quickly and in silence, under a cloud of worry. Before they left, Clara braided her hair, interlacing the plaits with dark purple ribbons. At the last moment she changed her mind and replaced them with her lucky bright pink ribbons.

"Clara, hurry! We're going to miss the bus."

She fumbled with the last ribbon as she kissed her father on the cheek.

"Don't forget your bag." He handed her the woven bag she had placed on one of the kitchen chairs the night before, now carrying the sketch of the two-headed dragon.

"Thanks, Papi. We'll see you tonight."

"Hurry, child!" Juana beckoned. "The bus is coming."

In the distance, Clara spotted the city bus rumbling down the potholed street.

A gray pigeon perched on the driver's side mirror. Long before anyone could remember, the pigeon had forged a bond with the rusted green-and-white vehicle rolling toward them. Some said the pigeon had been born in the bus and thought of it as their nest. Others believed the pigeon didn't realize it was a bird. The driver thought the pigeon fancied itself a sort of captain, riding their steed into battle every day, maneuvering around countless obstacles on their quest to lift the people of the city out of their daily doldrums. Hence, he took to calling the pigeon El Capitán. Everyone liked the driver's version best, so the name stuck.

"Buenos días." Juana smiled at the driver as she and Clara climbed up into the bus.

"Good morning," came the reply. "An early one for you two?"

Juana nodded but didn't explain. She led Clara to the first row of seats. When the bus passed their house, Clara spotted her father at the threshold. He waved to them, and Clara leaned out the window to wave back. A playful breeze tugged at the loose pink ribbon in her hair, carrying it off in a dance of color. She sat back and leaned her head on her mother's shoulder as El Capitán valiantly led the bus onward.

CHAPTER 9

IN WHICH LIFE AND DEATH

DISCUSS CAUSE AND EFFECT

Life and Death locked eyes on the bus as it rumbled past them.

"There she goes," Catrina said. "Off to meet her destiny."

Life chuckled. "I would say she's off to *make* her destiny."

The issue of free will was one the two friends often debated. At the heart of the debate was the question of choice: whether a person's destiny was determined by past events or if people had the ability to shape their own future.

Life believed that people created their own destiny. He argued that choices could be made freely, regardless of one's past experiences.

Catrina, on the other hand, argued that choice was an illusion. Free will was something people wanted, so they tricked themselves into thinking it was something they actually had. The truth, according to her, was that everything that happened in life was the natural and inevitable consequence of what came before, and it led—naturally and inevitably—to everything that followed.

"Like this." She displayed one of the many beaded bracelets wrapped around her bony wrist. "An unbroken chain of events. One leading right to another and another, and so on.

"People like to think they're in control," she went on. "But they're not. Whatever is bound to happen will happen, whether they like it or not."

She pointed at the deck of cards. "It's no different than you and me playing this game. We're not *choosing* the cards that determine the girl's fate; we are only *witnessing* the cards as they are played. And so it is with people. They are merely witnesses to their own destiny as it unfolds before them."

The clock in the Santo Domingo bell tower began to toll, an invitation to Mass. Dogs across the city responded with their own calls, and a flock of birds took flight.

"¡Mira!" a little boy called. He pointed at the bright pink ribbon clearly framed against the backdrop of wings temporarily blocking the sun. Had it been the darker purple ribbon, it would have escaped his attention entirely. As it was, the little boy jumped, reaching for the strip of pink.

"Careful!"

A man on a bicycle with a basket full of oranges swerved to avoid hitting the little boy. With a citrus-scented crash, the man and his fruit tumbled off the bicycle.

"See there?" Catrina indicated the little boy. "Cause . . ." Then she pointed at the rolling oranges. "Effect. One thing inevitably leads to another."

The oranges rolled gaily down the street. Life leaned over to pick one up, relishing the bright scent of the fruit's flesh. In his reverie, he didn't notice the curious bird that had landed on their table and was pecking at the deck of cards in the center.

The two friends watched the oranges and the continued effect they had on everyone who crossed their path: one man tripped, which made another man laugh, and that led to a heated argument between them; a cluster of dogs raced after another orange, running in front of a car and causing a small traffic jam; a street entertainer gathered as many oranges as he could and juggled them, to the great delight of a group of tourists, who tipped him for his efforts.

"All these lives were impacted by one stray ribbon, unspooling a series of events that were completely out of their control," Catrina said. "None of these people had any choice in what happened."

As she spoke, the bird took flight—unseen by the two friends as it carried away the top card of the pile, thus unfurling a different destiny for the girl on the bus.

"Everything is connected—you see?"

Catrina and Life turned back to the table.

"There is truth in what you say, of course." But Life knew there was more to the story.

"I can see you gathering your arguments." Catrina smiled. "Let's keep playing, and then you can tell me how I'm wrong."

"That I will." Life returned her grin and flipped over the next card. "FRESCO Y OLOROSO, EN TODO TIEMPO HERMOSO."

"Well, that's easy," Catrina said. "FRESH AND FRAGRANT, BEAUTIFUL IN ANY SEASON. It's the pine tree, of course!"

Neither friend found the pine tree on their tabla, so Life flipped over another card. "LA COBIJA DE LOS POBRES."

"That is the sun, THE BLANKET OF THE POOR," Catrina said.

"And still no bean for either of us."

Life flipped over a third card. "LAS JARAS DE ADÁN, DONDE PEGAN, DAN," he said.

"THE ARROWS OF ADAM STRIKE WHERE THEY HIT. That's rather cryptic," Catrina responded.

"Cryptic or not, I have it on my board!" Life placed his first black bean on the pictograph of the arrows.

Catrina laughed. "Well, I'm glad you're finally in the game." She placed a black bean counter on her tabla as well.

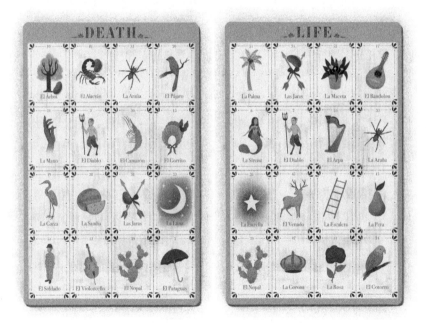

CHAPTER 10

"LAS JARAS"

anta María del Tule was a town that had sprouted around the enormous Árbol del Tule and the small chapel beneath its boughs. Almost everyone in Santa María del Tule worked in the tourist trade; those who didn't kept the town itself up and running. Eugenio could saw, nail, weld, paint, or build anything. Fidelia was equally skilled with needle and thread. Usmail and his wife, Carmelita, ran the bakery, which enveloped the town in the smell of fresh bread from sunrise to sunset. There was also a well-regarded doctor. However, most people consulted with Clara's aunt Chita first. She was known and beloved by all.

As if to prove the point, as soon as Juana and Clara

stepped off the bus, the clerk at the depot recognized them and waved them over. "Hola, Juana, Clara. Please tell Chita that Pablo's foot is completely healed," the clerk said. "I haven't been able to make it over there."

Juana told the clerk she'd relay the message.

A grocer along the way beckoned them into his store, where he gave Juana some guavas and a watermelon to take to Chita. "My stomach is back to normal." He patted his oversized belly.

The tortilla maker sent them on with a bundle of warm, freshly made tortillas; someone gave Juana a pair of shoes; and a young mechanic's apprentice rushed out, gushing with a story of a successful marriage proposal. "Please thank Chita for me! Her advice was perfect."

Juana laughed at the idea that her sister had moved from healing to counseling on matters of love. Still, she offered the boy her congratulations. "I'm sure Chita will be delighted to know."

Juana and Chita had grown up in a village on the outskirts of Oaxaca City. Chita was the eldest, and she had married young, leaving her family and moving to her husband's town, Santa María del Tule.

Chita had been lonely at first, and visited Juana and their parents as often as she could. But when her mother-in-law fell ill, Chita became the primary caregiver. By then she was already pregnant with her first child. As it turned out, she found a new friend in her mother-in-law, an ancient woman with weathered brown skin, silver plaits that hung down to her waist, and a profound love of all things living. She understood—intuitively—how things grew and flourished, which plants healed and which plants harmed, which herbs brought joy or sorrow or fear or love. She also had a magical garden with an unparalleled bounty of plants and flowers and trees that seemed to exist only in her domain.

Before she died, the old woman passed along her wealth of knowledge, teaching Chita everything she knew about the mysterious rules that governed the world of plants—and her plants, in particular. And so it was that Chita inherited her mother-in-law's love and skill. On the day her first son, Manolo, arrived, Chita's own garden sprouted all at once and in full bloom. It was her mother-in-law's blessing, and from that moment on Chita became the town healer.

"¡Ya llegamos!" Juana called out when they arrived at Chita's bright orange house.

A row of slender organ cacti leaned against the wall, and a lush purple-and-white bougainvillea plant spilled over the top of the house. Juana peered into her sister's window, a view that led right into a clean and colorful kitchen. "We're here!" she repeated.

"I'm in the back," Chita replied, and Clara and her mother followed the stone path beside the house out to Chita's garden.

Two fig trees heavy with fruit flanked the entrance to the path. Ceramic pots of various shapes and sizes lined the way. Some held tall and spiky cacti, while others boasted flowering plants with buds of yellow and orange; a pair of succulents grew in a rooster-shaped pot.

The path ended at a terrace with a few chairs and a table set beneath a pergola. Flowering vines crawled up and around the wooden posts that supported the roof of the pergola. Esteban sat at the table, peering under a small overturned box.

"What are you up to, little cousin?" Clara leaned over his shoulder.

Esteban looked up. He turned in his chair and wrapped his arms around Clara. "I'm so happy to see you!"

Clara hugged him back. "So, what's hiding under there?" She pointed at the box.

"A spider," Esteban said. "Did you know spiders can't see in the dark?"

"I didn't know that."

"But they can sense vibrations," Esteban went on. "That's how they get around."

"Interesting . . ."

"¡Hola, chicas!" Chita waved at Juana and Clara from the garden.

Her house was small and modest, but her garden was bountiful and gave the home the air of a grand estate. There were large agaves with fat and fibrous leaves, prickly pear cacti, and aloe plants. Cycads rose from the ground like giant pineapples with green head-dresses, interspersed between huajes, the trees from which Oaxaca got its name, with their fernlike leaves and long seedpods like enormous green beans.

Along the terrace, Chita had planted flor de mayo plants, with five-petal blossoms that resembled stars. Bees flitted dizzyingly between hibiscus flowers and bell-flowered dahlias as big as Clara's hand.

Of course, Chita grew herbs used for cooking, and there were all manner of fruit trees: guava, avocado, dragon fruit, plum, and lime. Many of these plants were native to Oaxaca and grew in all the local gardens. But Chita also had plants that came from other regions and thrived only in her garden: vanilla plants, cacao trees, achiotes with bright red thorny flowers.

There were plants that seemed unreal to Clara: jade-green vines that defied gravity, held aloft by blossoms that looked like butterfly wings; plants that produced perfectly spherical fruit with smooth, transparent skin; a tree no taller than Clara herself, with branches that extended horizontally and fruit that hung like drops. It was these very fruits that Chita was collecting when she waved Juana and Clara over.

"Welcome to your home," she said, her customary greeting.

Clara hugged her aunt.

"I'm glad you came," Chita told her, but her smile was framed by lines of worry.

"What is this?" Clara asked, pointing at the fruit in Chita's hand.

"Try it." Chita handed Clara one of the drop-shaped fruits. It was deep green, plump, and velvety soft. Clara held it up to her nose.

"It has no smell on the outside," Chita explained. "You have to bite into it."

As soon as Clara did, an explosion of flavor burst in her mouth.

"It smells like chocolate!" Juana exclaimed.

It tasted like chocolate, too, but there was a hint of something else.

"What is it?" Clara asked, wiping a drop of juice off her chin.

Chita smiled. "I call it chocanela."

"Chocolate-cinnamon!" Clara replied. "That's exactly what it is." She handed the fruit to Juana. "Try it."

"This is the first season the tree has yielded fruit," Chita explained. "I've been nurturing it for years."

"It's wonderful," Juana and Clara said in unison.

Chita laughed. "Well, let's get some of these bundled up for you to take home."

Chita handed Juana and Clara a basket each, laden with fruits and flowers. As they passed the table where Esteban sat, Chita gently admonished him.

"Esteban, you know very well we must honor all living creatures." She pointed at the box. "It is not our right to restrict anyone's freedom. We always pay a price for doing so."

Esteban sighed, but he lifted the box and released the spider.

"Here, give me a hand with this," Clara told her cousin, and she passed Esteban one of the chocanelas. The fruit fell and landed on the table with a soft splat. A small crack split the chocanela flesh, and a wave of chocolate and cinnamon wafted up toward them.

"Oops," Clara said.

"Ha! Better for us!" Esteban scooped up the fruit. "We get to eat that one for lunch." He followed Clara into the kitchen.

"Where are the boys?" Juana asked as she unpacked the food she had brought, as well as the gifts from the townspeople.

No sooner had the question been asked than Esteban's brothers bounded into the kitchen.

"¡Hola, Tía!" They each planted a kiss on Juana's cheeks and gave Clara a hug.

"We smelled your food," Manolo said.

"And the chocanela!" Victor added, grabbing a slice of fruit off the platter.

The boys got to work setting places for everyone, taking the food out to the terrace, adding a sparkling pitcher of green lemonade in the center. Beads of moisture dripped from the glass pitcher onto the table, creating a small puddle that Esteban's spider deftly avoided.

As they ate, Juana relayed the various messages she'd been given. Chita took her time explaining each case, and Esteban's brothers supplemented their mother's stories with silly faces and jokes. It wasn't long before Juana's anxiety vanished entirely.

Esteban, however, was immune to his mother's magic. His leg bounced nervously under the table, and he stared at Clara with an intensity she couldn't ignore.

"You're going to burn a hole right through me," Clara whispered. She reached out and tickled him. Esteban laughed, and for a brief moment the tension was broken.

"Aren't you hungry?" She looked at his plate. Esteban was not one to skip meals, especially when it involved Juana's food.

The boy shook his head.

"I know you're worried." She put an arm around him. "But I'm sure it's nothing." The words rang false between them. "Anyway, you should eat. You're starting to look like La Catrina!" She squeezed his arm and gave him another tickle.

Esteban's laughter released a growl of hunger, and with gratitude (for he truly did love to eat), he picked up his fork. Between mouthfuls, he told her about his friends and a new tongue twister he had learned. "Do you want to hear it?"

"Sure," she replied.

"*Tres tristes tigres, tragaban trigo en un trigal.*"

"What?" Clara burst out laughing. "'Three sad tigers gobbled up wheat in a wheat field.' What kind of tongue twister is that?"

"Try it!"

"You know I'm no good at tongue twisters." She didn't like seeming dumb in front of Esteban, as clumsy with her words as she was with everything else.

"Come on," he said. "You're always teaching me new things. Why can't I teach you this?"

"That's different."

"It isn't. Besides," he added, "I *know* you'll get it."

"Fine," she sighed. "I'll give it a try."

Esteban was a patient teacher, and for the next hour they nourished their bodies with food and their hearts with laughter as their tongues wrapped around silly words. In the garden the sun busily nourished the plants.

Somewhere buried deep in the folds of Clara's satchel, the dirt-colored scorpion with a black spot longed for nourishment, too. But he stayed put.

His time would come, and soon.

On the other side of town, a small boy unveiled a gift.

"Happy birthday, Adán," his parents said.

Adán gazed at the bow in his hands. It had been carved by his father. The wood was smooth and pliable; it felt cool to the touch. Engraved along the side were the words *Con Amor.*

A leather quiver held a handful of arrows made by his mother. The arrowheads were perfect triangles of obsidian—volcanic glass. The fletchings consisted of real feathers, soft and white. In the light, the arrows seemed to shimmer.

"Are they *magic*?" Adán asked, his eyes wide with the mystery of it.

"They were made with a great deal of love," his mother said. "Does that count as magic?"

Adán laughed. "Yes! Gracias," he said, and gave his parents a hug. "I love it!"

It had been a difficult year for this small family. They had lost a baby in the womb, and their home in an earthquake. Adán and his parents had no family in the area, and they had taken to sleeping in their truck until they could get back on their feet. Work was hard to come by; food and water, too. This bow and arrow, while small and simple, meant everything to Adán. It meant that no matter how difficult things got or how sad his parents were or how lonely he sometimes felt, the important things—like birthdays—still mattered.

"Can I go test it out?" Adán asked.

"Of course!" his father said. "But we need to go somewhere open, where you won't accidentally strike someone." He laughed.

The boy and his father walked out to a faraway field. The sun pulsed hot and bright upon them. But in the distance they could see darkness gathering. A drum of thunder rolled overhead.

"It looks like it's going to rain," the boy's father said. "Let's not go too far."

So they chose an open spot not too far, but far enough.

"Here?" Adán asked.

"Perfect," his father replied.

CHAPTER 11

IN WHICH
A PREMONITION UNFOLDS

After lunch, Chita, Esteban, Clara, and her mother walked to the tree. Clara's bag thumped rhythmically at her side, matching her rapid heartbeat. Their happy mood had quickly faded, and Juana's nervous tension coursed between them like an electric current. Even the sky seemed to respond, with distant flashes of light on the darkening horizon.

Clara had seen El Árbol del Tule dozens of times, but it never failed to impress her, with its massive crown of green foliage threatening to overtake the small church in its shadow. As a child, she used to believe it was a giant, enchanted to live out its days as a tree. She had felt sorry for the giant, whom she imagined to be pretty bored sitting there frozen for eternity. Between visits she would collect secrets—whispers of things said and overheard—that she would then spill into the tree, like small offerings.

For years, Clara believed the gnarly creatures shaped in the trunk were little gifts just for her, the tree's way of thanking her for the secrets. Eventually, she learned that they were simply a phenomenon of the tree's growth pattern. And yet, as she approached the tree, with Esteban at her side and her aunt and mother a few steps behind, Clara couldn't help but wonder if maybe . . . just maybe . . . there had been a shred of truth in her childhood belief.

As usual, tourists were gathered around the tree.

"This giant," the guide explained, "is nicknamed the Tree of Life because of the various life-forms you can see along its trunk." He pointed out the Lion, a bulbous formation with an uncanny resemblance to a lion's face framed by a wild mane. There was the Elephant, a fully formed baby pachyderm standing on the ground. The Crocodile was long and flat, appearing to crawl right out from under the roots.

"It's over here," Esteban whispered, pointing away from the group of tourists.

Clara's heart momentarily sped up. She took a deep breath.

I'm sure it's nothing.

Chita had kept up a steady stream of conversation during their walk in an effort to calm Juana. But as soon as Esteban pointed out the new creature, the two women fell silent.

The dragon was clearly visible and intricately detailed. The texture of the bark resembled scales and feathers. Small protrusions bubbled out of the dragon's two mouths like fire and ice, knots became claws, and a fibrous tangle of wood shaped the forked tail.

Esteban pointed out the small details Clara had included in her drawing: the *E,* the *C,* the ring.

"Do you see what I mean?" Esteban said.

Clara nodded, trying to still her now fiercely pounding heart.

"Can we see it?" Juana asked. "The drawing?"

Clara opened her bag and pulled out her sketchbook. She flipped to the page with the dragon sketch, a close approximation of the one that had gone missing.

Juana, Chita, and Esteban studied the picture. Clara didn't need to do that. She knew that the image on the tree was identical to the one she had made for Esteban.

"This," the tour guide said, standing directly behind them, "is the newest outgrowth that the tree has given us. Can anyone tell me what it is?"

He pointed at the formation of the dragon on the trunk. Some people tilted their heads, squinting as they studied the tree.

"It's a two-headed dragon," one of the tourists replied. Dressed in an elegant black suit and vest, with a red handkerchief poking out of his pocket, the man looked rather out of place. His beautiful companion nodded, and the group broke into collective head nodding and laughter.

"This is by far the most detailed and complex of the forms depicted on the tree," the guide went on, pointing out various aspects of the creature that Clara and Esteban had specifically chosen for the design.

It was at this very moment that the dirt-colored scorpion with a black dot decided to make its move.

Nestled among the pages of Clara's sketchbook, the scorpion had waited out the previous evening in Clara's kitchen. It had taken the bus ride to Santa María del Tule and sat through a lively lunch. Now it crawled out from its hiding spot and inched its way toward Clara's fingers, its stinger poised for attack.

"But there are dozens of other formations," the guide concluded. "Take this one here. . . ."

The guide was leading the tourists away when Clara felt a sharp pinch on her finger.

"Ow!" she cried, and dropped her sketchbook. Her finger throbbed sharply, and the pain quickly spread across her hand. An angry red spot on her finger appeared to be swelling.

"What happened?" Esteban asked.

"I don't know." Clara gasped as the pain in her hand intensified and spread up her arm. Her finger went numb. "I think something bit me."

Clara leaned over to pick up her book, and the ground seemed to sway beneath her. She stumbled and fell.

"Clara!" Juana cried, rushing to her side. "Are you okay?"

Clara sat up and blinked, trying to steady her vision. Everything seemed to be spinning around her. Her heart thrummed wildly in her ears.

"I'm . . . really . . . hot," she mumbled, reaching up to touch her forehead.

Chita spotted the wound on Clara's finger. She inspected it closely. "It's a scorpion sting!"

Chita turned to Esteban. "Run and ask the tour guide for some water and ice," she instructed. "Bring it here and stay with Clara. I'll be back in two minutes."

Esteban raced after the tour guide, but the telltale cramp of a premonition gripped his stomach, forcing him to a halt. He groaned and gulped in air, trying to keep from vomiting. He glanced back at Clara, leaning against her mother on the ground. Even from where he stood, he could see her skin shining with sweat, her chest rising and sinking unevenly. Ignoring the pain in his belly, he lumbered forward.

"Hello!" he called to the tour guide. "Excuse me!"

The guide turned and frowned.

A fresh wave of nausea arose, but Esteban fought it back.

"Are you okay?" the tour guide asked, running toward the boy.

Esteban nodded. "It's not me," he said between gasps. "It's my cousin. She was stung by a scorpion." He pointed at Clara, now lying on her mother's lap.

"What do you need?" the guide asked.

"Water and ice."

The tour guide sprinted to the bus, and a moment later he raced back with bottles of water and a small bag of ice. He took everything to Juana, who placed the ice on Clara's finger and urged her to drink water.

"Do you need anything else?" the guide asked Juana. "I can take you to the clinic."

"Thank you," Juana replied, forcing a smile. "My sister will be back any minute with the antidote."

"Good," he said. "I hope she feels better soon."

Juana nodded. She waited for the tour guide to move out of earshot before turning to Esteban.

"Is this it?" she asked. "Esteban, is this what your premonition was about?"

Esteban's stomach tightened.

"Is Clara going to die?" Juana's words were barely a whisper, but they echoed loudly in Esteban's ears.

"I—I don't know," he said.

Usually when Esteban witnessed his premonitions unfolding, a certainty fell upon him—the knowledge that no matter what he did, this event was coming to pass. It gave him comfort, relinquishing things to their ultimate destiny.

But what Esteban felt at that moment was not comfort; it was not the peace of resolution. What he sensed was the bitter onset of profound grief.

※

In the distance a rogue current of air split off from the gathering storm. Intoxicated by its newfound freedom, the wind went wild, raking through trees, whose branches bent and snapped; razing fields and demolishing fragile crops; snatching a little boy's arrow, a gift from the heart of one mother, and carrying it far away, into the heart of another.

Chita never saw it coming, the arrow. She had just stepped out of the house, her mind running through a checklist of ingredients she needed for the antidote. Clara would be fine; Chita was certain of it. Her skills would overcome Esteban's premonition. It was curious, though, how Esteban had been wrong about this premonition. That had never happened before.

The arrow struck a direct hit, and Chita instantly collapsed. Her last thought as she fell was surprise at the realization that this was the exact spot where her husband had been struck by lightning.

CHAPTER 12

IN WHICH LIFE
AND DEATH DISCUSS CHOICE
AND CONSEQUENCES

"A devastating consequence," Life sighed. They had set up their game a short distance from Chita's house and thus were present to witness the unfortunate event. Catrina had approached Chita and embraced her, welcoming her into her domain. A petal fell from Catrina's crown, but before it touched the ground, a violent gust of waterlogged wind yanked it away.

"If only that young boy had made a different choice," Life said. "If only he'd aimed his arrow in another direction."

"My friend," Catrina said. "You are mistaken to think anyone had a choice in this matter."

"Of course they did," Life replied. "The boy didn't have to stand where he did, he didn't have to—"

With a clap of thunder, the sky cracked open, releasing a downpour. Life raised his umbrella, expanding it to shield himself and his companion from the sudden onslaught of rain.

"You are assuming the boy had options," Catrina explained, "that he *chose* to stand where he did." She pointed at the water beginning to gather in rivulets down the street.

"See here—the path the rain is following is not arbitrary. It is entirely dependent on the shape and size of the cobblestones, the dirt or debris in its way, the particular slope of the street. It depends on many factors, some of which we cannot even perceive but all of which were in place long before the storm arrived."

"That's true, about the rain. But how does that apply to the boy and his arrow? Rain does not have free will. It couldn't choose a different path, even if it wanted to."

"And what does it mean to 'want' something?" Catrina asked. "Where does *that* desire originate?"

Life frowned as he pondered her question.

Catrina went on. "The boy's 'choice,' as you call it, was not arbitrary, nor was it made on a whim. It was based on a number of factors in place long before the moment he released his arrow."

"Such as?" Life asked.

"Well, perhaps the ground was rocky and the boy didn't have solid footing. Or maybe the ground was wet or too soft or smelled foul. Perhaps the sun was in his eyes or the grass too high upon his legs." Catrina shrugged. "There could be any number of factors, and the boy had no control over any of them. But like the stones on this street"—she pointed at the growing streams of water racing over the cobblestones— "those factors gradually nudged the boy until he found the spot, the only spot, from which he could shoot his arrow."

"So you're saying the result was inevitable."

"Yes!" Catrina nodded. "Inevitable, devastating though it is for the boy."

Just as quickly as it came, the rain ceased, and bright columns of light pierced the dark clouds, carving out blue patches of sky and casting rainbows over the town. Life and Death took a moment to admire the celestial canvas spread out before them.

"You make an intriguing point," Life finally said. "I will need to ponder that one for a bit."

Catrina motioned to the deck of cards. "In the meantime, shall we resume our game?"

Life obliged her and turned over the next card. "CON

LOS CANTOS DE SIRENA, NO TE VAYAS A MAREAR," he said, and he placed a black bean on the pictograph of a mermaid.

"Always wise advice." Catrina laughed. "DON'T BE SWAYED BY THE SONGS OF THE SIREN."

CHAPTER 13

IN WHICH
A HEART IS BROKEN

Huddled under the massive branches of El Árbol de Tule, Juana and Esteban had taken shelter from the rain. Clara lay on the ground with her head in her mother's lap.

The storm had come on suddenly and without warning. Almost as swiftly, Esteban's stomachache had vanished. But a new ache assaulted him.

The pain spread through him like so many fissures, shattering his body into a hundred pieces. The sharpness gradually dissipated, but it left behind a deep and unfamiliar darkness.

"I wonder where Chita is?" Juana muttered. She brushed a strand of hair off Clara's damp forehead. "She should be back by now."

Esteban wondered the same thing.

"Maybe she ducked indoors to wait out the rain," Clara said. Her finger ached painfully and her arm tingled, but the fever had subsided and her breathing was less erratic.

"No," Esteban said. "She wouldn't do that." His mother was a healer, and nothing ever stood in her way when she had a job to do.

The ache inside him hardened.

"Do you think—"

Juana's words were cut off by the sight of a woman racing toward the tree in the rain.

"Lupe!" Esteban jumped to his feet at the sight of his neighbor, a kind woman whose affinity for soap operas was rivaled only by her love for children.

Lupe was breathing heavily. Her clothes were wet and clung to her body.

"¡Ay, mi niño!" she cried, and she held out her arms to Esteban. "You poor boy!"

Esteban quietly walked into her rain-soaked embrace, not knowing why he did it but knowing simply that he had to. Through the thin cloth that separated them, Esteban could hear her heart beating a sorrowful tune.

"Lupe?" he asked. "Why are you crying?"

The woman took a deep breath and let the words come with her tears. "It's your mother," she said. "I can't explain it."

"What is it?" Juana asked.

"She's . . ."

The unspoken word hung heavily in the air before them. There were things one knew without needing to be told.

Esteban's legs gave way, and the ache inside him grew ravenous, eagerly devouring that very space where love used to reign.

CHAPTER 14

"LA SIRENA"

"Esteban?" Clara looked over at her little cousin. It had been hours since Lupe's tearful revelation at the tree. Her body had overcome the scorpion venom, and the effects of the sting had mostly worn off. She still had a dull ache in her finger, and a much heavier ache in her heart.

Clara's throat was raw from crying; her eyes, swollen from grief. Esteban, on the other hand, had not shed a tear or released even a single sob. Clara was pretty sure he hadn't even blinked since Lupe brought them back to her house.

"I want to see her," he had said when Lupe finally explained what happened.

"No," Juana had told him. "That's not how she would want you to remember her."

"But I need to make sure," he said. "I think there's been a mistake."

Lupe hugged him then. "No, mi hijo," she said. "There's no mistake."

Esteban knew Lupe was right. The emptiness inside him confirmed what his premonition had told him. Something very bad had happened.

And so Esteban stayed with Lupe and Clara for the next few hours, remembering his mother as he wanted to remember her, while Juana and the rest of the family made the necessary arrangements for Chita's burial and send-off.

Years ago, after the suddenness of Esteban's father's death had taken Chita by surprise, she vowed to never again let death knock them off their feet, and had left explicit instructions about what to do in the event of her own demise. She had two requests.

First, Manolo was to be the head of the household, responsible for the care of his younger siblings. But he would not be alone or unprepared. For years, Chita had set aside what little money she could to help provide for the boys until they could provide for themselves. It was not a fortune, but it would be enough, and the community would chip in to help. As the youngest, Esteban would move in with Clara's family until he was old enough to rejoin his brothers.

Chita's second request was that sadness not be allowed to enter her home. Instead, there would be a party, with food and music and dancing. Everyone she knew and loved was invited. Preparations for the lively celebration were already being made as Esteban stared unblinkingly into Lupe's living room.

"You should eat something," Clara told him. "It'll make you feel better."

On the table beside him was a plate with a barely nibbled concha—a round doughy roll topped with a crumbly coat of sugar. Lupe had also given him a glass of milk and some quesadillas, all of which stood untouched on the table.

"I'm not hungry," he said.

"What about a sweet?" Clara asked. "These are your favorite." She reached for one of the hard candies wrapped in colorful paper that Lupe always kept in bowls around her house. Her hand accidentally knocked over the bowl, scattering colorful candies across the floor.

"Maybe later," Esteban said, and Clara tucked the sweet into her pocket before collecting the others and returning them to their place.

"Well . . . how about this?" Clara said. "I've been working on it for a while."

She pointed at a page in her sketchbook where she had drawn a winged horse.

"You can have it," she added.

Esteban didn't even glance at it. His eyes were fixed on the door, his body poised to spring up from the couch. "Do you hear that?" Esteban's body stiffened; his eyes were bright and alert.

"Hear what?"

"That song."

Clara leaned forward. She heard a jumble of words from a faraway radio, but no song. Lupe was on the phone in the kitchen. A dog barked sporadically.

"No," she replied. "What song is it?"

Esteban trembled.

"What is it?" Clara asked. She rose and put her arms around him. Waves of cold rippled off his skin.

"*No me olvides, amor,*" Esteban whispered.

> *Nunca estoy lejos de ti.*
> *Tu vida ha sido un dulzor,*
> *Un regalo para mi.*

Clara's throat tightened as she recognized the words.

"That's impossible. . . ." But before she could say anything else, Esteban was at the door.

"Wait!" Clara called, and she caught up with him. "Are you sure it's not in your imagination? I can't hear a thing."

"It's faint, but I can definitely hear it!" His face glowed, as if lit from within. He smiled broadly, and Clara could actually see the sorrow release its grip on him.

"It's her," he whispered. "She's okay!" He reached for the door handle. "She's calling me."

Esteban yanked the door open. "Mami!" he cried. No sooner had the word left his lips than it fell with a heavy thud at the threshold.

There was no Chita—not a soul around, not even a sound.

Esteban frowned and peered down the street, looking one way, then the other.

"Esteban . . ." Clara gently took his hand, but he pulled away and walked out of the house.

"Mami?" he asked. This time the precious word was barely a whimper.

"It's not Chita," Clara said. She put her hand on his arm.

"I *heard* her!" He yanked his arm away. "I know it is! She's back home waiting for me."

Before Clara could respond, Esteban was racing away.

"Esteban!" Clara chased after him.

"Mami!" The boy's cries trailed behind him as he rushed toward his home.

"Hey," Clara called out. "Esteban, wait!" She picked up her pace. Esteban picked up his pace as well.

Clara was fast, but just as she was about to reach her cousin, he pushed himself forward and out of her grasp. He ran heedlessly, quickly approaching a busy corner.

"Stop!" she cried, sprinting after him. "Don't go into the street!"

The light ahead turned yellow and would be red by the time Esteban hit the corner. At his speed, he wouldn't be able to stop in time.

Clara forced herself to pump her legs faster, quickly closing the distance between her and Esteban. As she had predicted, the light turned red at the moment he stepped off the sidewalk. Clara reached for his shirt, barely grabbing the collar and pulling him back just in time. A car honked at them, zooming past. The honk startled a dog on a leash, and it chased the car down the street, dragging its owner behind it.

Esteban landed on Clara with such force that it took her breath away. But she instinctively reached up and wrapped her arms around him. As she gulped for air, she felt his heart pounding. His body was otherwise still, and he wasn't squirming out of her grasp.

"Are you okay?" she gasped.

Esteban nodded, blankly staring at the sputtering cars, buses, and motorcycles rumbling past them on the street.

"What were you thinking?" she said. "You could have been killed."

The cracks in Esteban's heart gave way beneath the weight of his sadness. Clinging to Clara and drowning in sorrow, he finally cried.

"It's okay," she whispered. "It's okay to cry."

She held him for a long time before helping him to his feet. Then, with his hand clasped tightly in hers, she walked him back to Lupe's house.

At the threshold of the house, she leaned down so that they were at eye level. "Esteban, I want you to know something very important."

"What is it?" he asked.

She squeezed his hand tightly. "I will never let anything bad happen to you."

"Promise?" His word was so fragile that Clara almost missed it.

"Promise." She held out her pinkie in the universal sign of commitment.

Esteban wrapped his pinkie around hers, sealing the deal.

That evening, Chita's home filled with people who had come to share their love and food, their music and laughter. To Esteban and his grieving brothers they also gave hugs and words of comfort. The night went long, with neighbors and friends bringing gifts to honor the woman who had healed their hearts and bodies countless times. Clara stayed by her little cousin until he was too tired to stand. Then she led him to his room and tucked him into bed. He didn't stir an inch.

It would be many hours before the house was empty and tidied up, the dishes cleaned. Clara went around the garden, blowing out all the candles. In the darkness she accidentally kicked over one of Chita's small planters.

When the house was all closed up, Clara and Juana made their way to bed. Clara had set up a pillow and blanket for herself on the floor next to Esteban's bed. Her mother had suggested Clara sleep with her in a proper bed, rather than on the hard floor. But Esteban had begged her to keep him company that night, and Clara had made a promise. What good was a promise if you kept it only when it was convenient?

The floor in Esteban's room *was* hard and very

uncomfortable, the pillow was flat, the thin blanket offering as much warmth as an open window. Nevertheless, sleep quickly overtook her, and Clara's discomforts soon vanished.

She fell so deeply into her slumber that she didn't hear Esteban tossing in his bed and crying out.

She didn't notice when he awoke and sat up in bed.

She didn't feel the cold breeze that snuck into the room from the open window.

Nor did she hear the song that filled the room.

> *No me olvides, amor.*
> *Nunca estoy lejos de ti.*
> *Tu vida ha sido un dulzor,*
> *Un regalo para mi.*

Had Clara looked up just then, she would have seen Esteban crawling out of the window, eager in his determination to follow the music. She would have wondered at the lantern, floating in the garden in midair, led by what appeared to be an invisible hand. She would have cried out for him to stop as he trailed behind the light deeper into the garden.

But, alas, she saw none of that.

Clara did, however, hear Esteban's cry as he tripped on the planter that she had knocked over earlier that

evening. When he fell, his cry broke through her dreams, and she immediately shot up.

"Esteban?" The room was cold and breezy. Goose bumps rose along her arms.

"Esteban?" Clara scanned the room, looking for her cousin. A flicker caught her eye, and she peered out into the garden, at the giant cactus towering in the night, framed by a shimmering halo of light.

"Esteban!" she cried as her cousin walked into the shimmering plant and vanished.

CHAPTER 15

IN WHICH A PROMISE
IS A PROMISE

"Wait!" Clara jumped out of the window and sprinted to the prickly nopal. She was sure her eyes were playing tricks on her, and yet Esteban was nowhere to be seen. The night was silent but for the thrum of crickets and her heart racing in her ears.

"Esteban!" she whispered into the night. "Where are you?"

A faint sound—almost imperceptible—reached her, and she closed her eyes, forcing herself to listen.

Amor.

"Love?" she wondered aloud. "Who's there?" She walked around the nopal.

Lejos de ti.

The words were distant and seemed to be moving

farther away, but Clara knew what she was hearing. She closed her eyes again, slowly stepping in the direction from which the words seemed to originate.

Tu vida . . . dulzor.

She moved closer.

Un regalo.

Closer.

"Para mi," she whispered, and opened her eyes.

There were two things Clara was certain about. First, Esteban had been right—it *was* Chita's voice. Second, the song was coming from inside the cactus.

Cautiously, Clara extended her hand toward the nopal's rough and prickly skin. She expected to feel a hard and unyielding surface. Instead, the nopal gave way easily to the pressure of her finger, as if it were made of gooey rubber. Even the sharp thorns, glinting brightly in the moonlight, were flexible and malleable to her touch. She pushed harder, but the plant only stretched further.

Clara stepped back and pulled her hand away. The nopal recovered its shape.

She had been in Chita's garden many times, and she had received her fair share of scratches from this very nopal whenever she'd had to pluck the sweet prickly pear fruit off its meaty leaves. This stretchy phenomenon was not normal.

"Esteban?" she called out again. There was no answer, but Clara noticed that the music was fading.

She pushed against the spines once more. This time the plant seemed a bit stiffer, more resistant to her touch, as if it were transforming back to its original form. If she didn't act soon, she would lose Esteban. She had promised to take care of her little cousin, and he trusted her to keep her word.

"Okay," she said, and took one definitive step forward. The nopal was rough and coarse now as she pushed against it, but still it gave way. She took another step, walking deeper into the cactus, feeling as if she were bearing down against a rubber wall. She continued to move forward until an opening began to spread apart in the nopal, growing into an elongated vertical gash.

Through the opening Clara could see a sunlit scene of tall trees and ropy vines dangling from branches, orchids clinging to the trunks of trees, and thick banana-shaped leaves reaching up from the ground.

"What is this place?" she asked, taking a final step.

A sound like air being sucked out of a room followed at her heels. A sudden change of pressure made her feel dizzy and light-headed. She turned around quickly, thinking to retrace her steps, but instead of Chita's garden there was only a dense jungle, spreading out in every direction as far as the eye could see. Even the cactus was gone.

Clara's chest tightened, unable to contain her racing heart, as a deep foreboding pooled in her stomach.

CHAPTER 16

IN WHICH LIFE AND DEATH
DISCUSS INEVITABILITY

"So there's a flaw in your theory," Life said. The sky had cleared and a veil of stars fanned over their heads as their second day came to an end. Chita's guests and mourners had long departed; the house was shrouded in silence.

In the bright moonlight, Catrina had been stitching a new set of flowers onto her dress. It was a hobby she had taken up years ago to pass the hours during their game. After centuries of games, her embroidery had evolved into a fine art.

"Go on," she said.

"You talk about the boy not having a choice in where and how he shot his arrow, but I don't think it's as black and white as all that."

Catrina grinned as she continued stitching.

"All the factors you mentioned," Life explained, "the rocky soil, the foul smell, the tall grass . . . It isn't inevitable that those things would affect the boy. He could easily have chosen to ignore them."

"Very clever, my friend." Catrina tapped on her skull. "And you are right, of course. However . . ." She paused, giving Life a moment to acknowledge he was about to be bested. "Whether the boy chooses to be bothered is certainly not a decision he makes out of the blue. Like everything else, it, too, depends on what has happened in his life leading up to that moment."

"For instance?" Life asked.

"Perhaps he's had a bad experience with rocky terrain before. Maybe he fell. Or he was bitten by a snake hiding in the tall grass."

A lone dog howled in the night, and a cloud of bats streaked across the sky.

"I understand your point," Life replied. "But to say he has no choice in *anything* he does . . . Why, that suggests *nobody* can ever be responsible for their actions. Surely that's not what you believe?"

"How could they be responsible for something that is out of their control?"

Catrina's needle glowed in the moonlight. With a quick knot and deft tug of the orange thread, she finished a bouquet of marigolds on her dress. She slipped the needle and thread into her skirts.

"Well . . . people have both reason and imagination," Life said.

Catrina looked up. "Meaning what?"

"The boy Adán may have suffered a fall upon rocky terrain, but he can *reason* that this does not mean he will always fall."

"I see," said Catrina.

"And," Life went on, "he can *imagine* a way to protect himself from snakebites—perhaps rubber boots."

Not having eyebrows, Catrina was unable to frown or squint or show any form of displeasure through her facial features. But Life was used to reading her emotions in more subtle ways, and he knew that she was not happy about the crack forming in her theory. Life suppressed his grin and went on. "As long as a person has reason and imagination, then they can choose whether to be influenced by their past or not. Isn't that free will?"

Catrina tapped her long, bony fingers on the table. "Well!" she said.

Life had temporarily gained the upper hand in their debate; however, he knew better than to gloat. This conversation was far from over, and already he had spotted some loose threads in his theory. He was certain Catrina would unravel them soon.

In the meantime, the game had to continue. Life picked up the deck of cards. "Ready?" he asked.

Catrina nodded, and Life flipped over the top card. "ME LO DAS O ME LO QUITAS," he said.

"GIVE IT TO ME OR TAKE IT FROM ME," Catrina replied. "You know, I've never understood that riddle. How is that a melon?"

"It's a play on words," Life explained. "The first four letters of the riddle spell out the first four letters of the word: *m-e-l-o*."

Catrina nodded. "Of course! I see that now. Though, unfortunately, I do not see the image on my tabla."

"Nor do I," Life added. He flipped over the next card. "PÓRTATE BIEN CUATITO, SI NO TE LLEVA EL COLORA-DITO." Life chuckled as he recited the riddle for the new card.

"BEHAVE YOURSELF, LITTLE BUDDY, OR THE RED ONE WILL TAKE YOU AWAY." Catrina nodded. "Enter the devil."

She drew out each word as she spoke it, and she placed a bean on the pictograph of the red devil.

"Things are starting to get interesting," Life murmured, placing a bean on his tabla as well.

"Things always get interesting when the devil makes an appearance," Catrina replied.

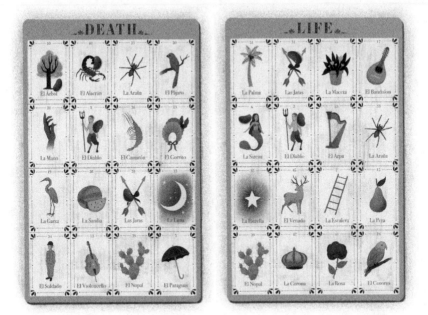

CHAPTER 17

"EL DIABLO"

El Diablo

The air was wet and heavy, laced with something Clara could only identify as "green." Her skin glistened with a thin layer of sweat. The ground beneath her feet was soft and cushiony. She bent down to touch it, running her fingers along what felt like a bed of moss. Above, a symphony of birds called to each other, their tunes tangled up with the rustling of leaves and the almost inaudible high-pitched buzz of heat.

"Where am I?"

Clara had never traveled far beyond Oaxaca City, so this unfamiliar environment was a novelty to her. Her mind spun with theories about how it got to be in Chita's backyard.

Maybe this is where she gathered her special herbs.

But that didn't make sense. Chita would have told Juana—there were no secrets in the family. Indeed, Chita would have *shown* them this world.

Maybe I'm dreaming.

Clara pinched her arm until a sharp pain bit through her.

Maybe I'm just imagining things.

But the tangled morass around her was rich and detailed.

Though she couldn't explain it, there was no way her imagination could have conjured a place like this. She had just stepped through a cactus into another world. And Esteban was somewhere in this world as well.

"Esteban!" she called out. "Where are you?"

The jungle responded in a rustle of plants and chattering birds. A frog croaked nearby. Everywhere there was water and green and the heavy weight of dread.

I need to find help.

"Help!" she cried. "Somebody, please help!"

A hot gust of wind washed over her. Her heart thrummed heavily in her chest.

What if there's nobody here?

"Hello?" she called out again. The word lodged itself in her tight throat. "Help?"

There was no help.

"Okay." She took a breath.

"Okay." She pushed down the panic crawling up her throat.

I can do this. I just need to focus.

She took another breath and slowly released the air in her lungs. She had told Esteban she would take care of him, and she would be true to her word.

I will find him.

Clara squared her shoulders and gave her heart a chance to settle into a more manageable rhythm. A third breath.

The jungle was dense and nearly impassable. There was no trace of other people, at least not that she could see.

"I need a better view!"

Armed with that thought, Clara approached the nearest tree, intent on climbing it. However, its gray trunk was far too smooth and offered no solid footholds. Another tree proved equally impossible. As she looked about, she noticed that all the trees were the same: gray and smooth and useless for climbing. Vines hung from the branches, but they were too high and out of reach.

"Esteban!"

The jungle carried his name a great distance, and replied in rustles and wafts of dampness.

Shaking her hands to relieve some of her nervous energy, Clara pondered her options.

"Right. How do I get up?"

"I know!" a voice croaked in response.

"Who's there?" Clara spun in place as she scanned the trees and underbrush.

"I am! I am!" the voice replied. "Down here."

Clara looked down at a fiery orange frog jumping beside her foot.

A talking frog?

She shook her head. "I'm going crazy!"

Keeping an eye out for a tree that would allow her to gain some height, Clara made her way deeper into the jungle. The orange frog kept pace with her, jumping alongside her shoe.

"These trees are so strange," Clara said, speaking aloud in an effort to keep her fear at bay. "They don't even look like they're real."

A few times she stopped and attempted to climb one, but with nothing for her hands or feet to grip, she simply slid down the trunk.

"There *must* be a way up," she said.

"I know! I know!" the frog croaked again.

Clara stopped. The frog stopped with her.

"Did you . . ."

She paused.

"I did! I did!" The frog jumped excitedly, a flash of orange, up and down.

Clara peered more closely at the small amphibian at her feet.

"No," she whispered.

"Yes, yes, yes."

The orange frog's jumping became more wild and erratic.

"Is this some kind of trick?" Clara looked around. "What's happening?"

"No trick, no trick."

"But you're . . . talking."

"Yes!" came the response. The frog stopped jumping.

"How is that possible?" Clara said. She straightened up. "Where exactly am I?"

"Asrean!" the frog replied, its voice deep and reverential.

"Asrean?"

She had heard about Asrean, but only in whispers and rumors. It was supposed to be a place of unlimited beauty and abundant natural resources, a hidden paradise.

"But that's just wishful thinking," she said. "Isn't it?"

"Real, real, real," the frog said, jumping all around her feet.

"Wait a minute." Clara studied the trees, noting how the light glinted off their shiny gray trunks, trunks that looked almost as if they were made of metal.

She ran her fingers across the bark of the nearest tree. When she flicked her finger against the surface, it produced a sharp metallic clink. The tree was definitely not made of wood.

"What is this?" she asked.

"Silver, silver, silver!" the frog croaked.

"Silver!" Clara gazed at all the trees around her. There were dozens—hundreds!—of towers of pure silver reaching high up into a lush canopy of green. "That's incredible."

She turned her attention to the vines. From afar, they looked green, but on closer inspection it was obvious they were a tight weave of bronze. The leaves on the trees were velvety soft and smelled like rain.

"Wait a minute!" She pulled away. "If Asrean is real and has always been in Chita's garden, then how come I've never seen it? There's no way Chita would have kept this world to herself."

"No, no, no." The frog jumped from leaf to leaf, a spot of orange on green. "A door was opened."

"A door? What? Why? How?"

The frog jumped onto a leaf at eye level with Clara.

"El Diablo," the frog said, its voice hushed but heavy.

A cold gust of wind crept up Clara's back.

"He opened a passage," the frog added. "Between the worlds."

A knot unraveled in Clara's stomach, releasing a sickening sensation through her body. "Who is El Diablo? And why did he open a passage?" She looked around. "And where is Esteban?"

"I know! I know! I know!" the frog said.

"So tell me!" Clara cried.

"First things first," the frog replied.

"What does that mean?"

"You give me something. I give you help."

"*What?*"

"There are rules in a place like this," the frog croaked. "Nothing is free."

"But I don't have anything to give you," Clara replied.

The frog jumped onto a raindrop-shaped leaf.

"Okay, then. Bye-bye." Swiftly it sprang onto another leaf and then another, quickly jumping out of sight.

"Wait!" Clara chased after the frog. "Please help me. I'm totally lost here."

The frog stopped. "You give me something. I give you help."

"Something like what?" Clara asked, catching her breath.

"What do you have?"

Clara put her hands in her pockets. She pulled out a scrap of paper with a few words cut off—the remains of a grocery list. She held the paper out to the frog.

"No." The frog jumped to another leaf, and Clara followed it.

"Do you want a paper clip?"

The frog contemplated the twisted piece of shiny metal but passed on that as well.

"Oh!" Clara said. "What about this?" She pulled out the small hard candy she'd offered Esteban earlier. Already that seemed like ages ago.

"Ooh!" the frog sighed. "Pretty, pretty, pretty."

"It's a sweet," Clara said. "You eat it." She held the candy out to the frog. "Do you want it?"

"Yes, yes, yes."

Clara unwrapped the candy and set it on the leaf next to the frog.

In one gulp, the frog swallowed the round ball. It belched, and a spray of blue dots blossomed on its orange skin. "Pretty, pretty, pretty!"

"Yes," Clara replied. "It *is* pretty. Now can you help me?"

"Yes!" The frog croaked. "Follow me."

Clara ran after the frog. "Where are you going?"

The spot of orange moved chaotically, leading Clara—jump by jump—to a small clearing.

In the middle of the clearing one tree towered over all the others. An old and rickety ladder, blanketed in moss, rested against the trunk.

"Where did this come from?" Clara asked.

"The hunters," the frog croaked.

"Hunters? Where are they? Maybe they can help!"

But the frog was already halfway up the ladder.

"Hey!" Clara called out. "Wait up!"

The ladder looked unstable; a few rungs were scattered on the ground, and others were bent at precarious angles.

The frog urged her on. "Hurry, hurry, hurry."

Clara took a breath and put her hand on one of the rungs and her foot on another. As soon as she stepped up, the rung snapped beneath her weight.

"Um . . . I don't think it's sturdy enough," she told the frog, but it was no longer in sight. All she could see was the ladder disappearing into a massive cluster of branches and leaves overhead.

"Hello?"

The fear in her voice reflected a single thought.

I can't do it.

Clara released her grip on the ladder and stepped back. There had to be another way.

Seconds ticked by, turning into minutes. The jungle heat seemed to settle more heavily upon her, as did the weight of her indecision.

"See here!" the frog beckoned from a height beyond sight. "Look, look, look! Hurry!"

The frog's sense of urgency was alarming, and Clara approached the ladder once more. Whether she liked it or not, she was Esteban's only hope, and this ladder seemed to be the only chance of finding him.

Her hands gripped the mossy wood, and she stepped onto another rung. This time the rung held, and she tentatively began her climb.

The ladder shook and wobbled. More than once a rotted rung collapsed, and Clara had to wrap her arms around the tree to keep from falling. Still, she continued her ascent.

"Don't look down," she whispered. "Or to the side."

She kept her gaze pinned to the rung directly above her hand: one after another until she ran out of rungs and there were only branches.

The orange frog was waiting for her. A wave of relief flooded over her when she spotted the only familiar creature in this jungle.

The frog had crawled onto a thick silver branch, and Clara followed suit, keeping her arms and legs wrapped tightly around the bough. Jump by jump, squirm by squirm, the frog and Clara made their way to the end of the branch.

Once there, Clara was glad she had risked the climb, for she could finally see what she needed to see.

The surrounding jungle was vast and dense, flaunting every imaginable shade of green. In one direction, snowcapped mountains lined the horizon. In another, the trees gave way to a lake reflecting the sky, as clear and flawless as a sheet of glass.

"There!" the frog croaked.

Clara looked toward where the frog was pointing. For a moment she saw only more jungle. Then she noticed what appeared to be a stone structure peeking out from among the treetops.

"Go there," the frog said, and it leaped off the tree.

"Wait!"

Clara's request plunged after the frog, getting lost in the foliage below.

"Okay, then," she whispered, closing her eyes to stop her head from spinning. "I *can* do this. Esteban needs me."

With her resolve in place, Clara opened her eyes and made the uneasy descent. She slipped only once, but fortunately it was near the bottom and the soft mossy ground broke her fall.

A sense of direction had never been one of Clara's strengths, and she was often getting lost in neighborhoods she'd known her whole life. So she took extra time to think about her location and where she needed to go.

The stone structure was directly to the left of the enormous tree. As long as she could keep the tree in her sight, she'd find her way.

"Good," she whispered, and without giving herself a second to change her mind, she set off toward the stone structure.

CHAPTER 18

IN WHICH WE LEARN ABOUT
THE KINGDOM OF LAS POZAS

Every few steps, Clara would turn to make sure the tree was in sight. The dense foliage threatened to block her view, but she checked her location time and again, not moving until she knew exactly where she was relative to the tree.

The brush at her feet was a mesh of green that tangled and tripped her up, but still she trudged onward. The heat became stifling, and a desperate thirst fell upon her.

A promise is a promise.

Reciting the words until they became a mantra, Clara made slow but steady progress. A few times she had to backtrack, she tripped more than once, and her fear never left her side. But she pushed on through the endless sea of green until she came upon a web of vines so dense and tightly knit they formed an impenetrable wall.

"Now what?"

And that was when she heard it: Esteban's voice.

"Is Mami there?"

The words were clear and so close! Clara was certain Esteban was on the other side of the vines. She was about to call out to him when a man's voice replied.

"Yes," he said. "She's been waiting for you."

Clara did not recognize the voice, but it made every hair on her arms stand on end.

"Come," the man went on. "It's just up ahead."

Clara strained to see through the wall of vines. She thrust her hands into the mesh, tugging the vines aside until she opened a slit big enough to spot her little cousin. A tall man in a red suit held Esteban's hand. The two walked toward a stone circle atop a hill.

Clara had no idea who the man was or where they were going, but she knew he was lying to Esteban, and every cell in her body vibrated on high alert.

As adrenaline flooded her bloodstream, she tried to widen the opening she had made in the hedge. Briars tore at her clothes, scratching and poking her exposed flesh. But the vines were so tightly intertwined that she had to give up.

Through the gap she saw Esteban and the man cresting the hill.

Next Clara tried to climb the wall, but when she searched for a foothold, the vines became so loose and slack they wouldn't hold her weight.

"What is going on?" she cried. It was almost as if the vines were enchanted.

Esteban and the man moved farther away, and her heart sank.

Desperately, she called out to him. "Esteban!"

The boy stopped and looked directly at the vines behind which Clara fought to be seen. For a moment she was sure he spotted her. But then the man in red leaned down and whispered something in his ear. Esteban quickly turned away.

Before they walked off, the man looked back. The jungle behind Clara fell silent, and a finger of ice ran up her spine.

The man's eyes found hers, locking on to them. In that instant her breath fled her body, turning to frost upon contact with the air. Unable to blink, Clara teared up, and for a moment her heart simply stopped beating.

Then the man broke eye contact and walked away. The cacophony of jungle life exploded around her. Clara's heart raced erratically beneath her shirt, already drenched in sweat.

"Esteban . . ." The whispered word fell from her lips and shriveled on the ground.

It took a moment for the chill to leave Clara's body, and longer still for her brain to thaw. She had no idea what was going on, but without a doubt—the man in red was up to no good.

A renewed urgency coursed through her veins as she scanned the wall for an opening. She walked first to the left, testing out different potential gaps, until the wall abruptly dropped off on a sheer cliff. At the bottom, the crowns of enormous trees swayed in a breeze.

She ran back to her starting point and followed the towering vines to the right this time, walking until she found herself on the edge of another cliff, looking down on the very same large trees.

"*No!*" Clara cried.

She was certain now that some kind of magic was keeping her out.

Or trapping Esteban in.

"But if *they* got in," she said, "there must be a way!"

A flutter of feathers popped out from the hedge. A tiny bird cocked its head at Clara and chirped.

She looked back at the bird.

"Can you . . ."

That's silly. Birds can't talk.

"Can I what?" the bird asked.

"You can!" Clara exclaimed.

First the talking frog, now the bird. The strangeness of this world only fed Clara's growing unease. And yet the frog had been able to help. Perhaps the bird could help, too.

"I need to get to the other side," she told the bird. "Do you know how I can do that?"

The bird chirped, then said, "You need to ask the guardians of Las Pozas."

"Las Pozas? Where can I find it?"

"It's the kingdom beyond the hedge."

The bird squeezed itself into a gap in the vines. From within the jumble of greenery it continued, "That's where the boy is going."

"And the guardians?" Clara peered into the hedge. "Where are they?"

"I can tell you." The bird stopped and plucked at a berry.

"Please do!" Clara cried.

"What can you give me in exchange?"

"Give you?" Clara remembered what the frog had said about the rules of Asrean. "Ugh! I gave away my last candy." She turned out the pockets of her pants.

The bird waddled out of its nook in the vines and stared at Clara before releasing a dismissive tweet. "Silly girl! What would I do with your pockets?"

"I'm not offering you my pockets," Clara shot back. "I'm just showing you that I don't have anything to give."

The bird ducked into the foliage. "Too bad!"

"But I need your help." Clara followed the bird as it wove through the vines, plucking at berries and insects along the way. "I need to get to my cousin. He's in trouble."

"He probably is," the bird replied. It nibbled on a berry, then added, "Are you good at anything? Can you sing? I've always wanted a good song."

Clara shook her head. "I'm terrible at singing."

"Pity, pity," the bird chirped. "Can you dance?"

"No, and I can't cook or sew or even tell good jokes!" She didn't wait for the bird to respond. "Please, can't you just tell me how to get through?" Her voice was loud and laced with anger.

"*Chit, chit, chit.*" The bird buried itself deeper into the tangle of vines.

Clara briefly lost sight of it, but then the bird suddenly popped back out farther down the wall.

"Can you draw?" the bird asked. "Could you draw me a horn?"

"A horn?"

"Yes!" The bird chirped gaily. "Like a unicorn horn: swirly and covered with diamonds, but instead of being pointy, it bends at the top and ends in a hook with a basket for all my berries." The bird bowed. "And make it small enough for my head."

"That sounds really complicated. And besides, how would a drawing fit on your head?"

"Not a drawing," the bird chirped. "I can make it real!"

"How?" Clara asked.

The bird laughed. "You don't know anything!"

"I'm not from here—okay?" Clara said. "And I need your help."

The bird flew to the ground at Clara's feet. "You

draw a unicorn horn. If I like it, it'll become real, and I will help you."

"And if you don't like it?"

"Then I won't help you."

Clara considered her options. "The thing is," she began, "I'm really not such a good drawer. . . ."

"Too bad!" With a flutter of its tail and a flap of wings, the bird caught a breeze. "Bye-bye!"

"Wait!" Clara ran after it. "Come back. I'll do it! I'll draw your horn!"

But the bird had left, and Clara's words drifted aimlessly away.

A sinking feeling overtook her as she realized her moment of insecurity might have cost Esteban his life.

CHAPTER 19

IN WHICH DEATH
PRESENTS A GIFT AND
A WINNING ARGUMENT

he din and commotion of the midnight market in downtown Oaxaca City filled the air. Tucked into a corner, Life and Death sat at a stone table with the remnants of a chessboard painted on its surface. For centuries, old men, and more than a few women, had gathered at this and other tables like it to share strategies, stories, and plenty of gossip through the night. Over time, the chessboard surfaces had been worn down from countless elbows and multiple cleanings. Now only a few checkered spots could be seen.

Life had set up their game on one of these surfaces. The circle of glass through which they had a window into Clara's journey sat on the table between them. Next to it was the deck of remaining cards, facedown.

Life flipped the top card over. "NO TE ARRUGUES, CUERO VIEJO, QUE TE QUIERO PA' TAMBOR."

"DON'T YOU WRINKLE, DEAR OLD LEATHER, SINCE I WANT YOU FOR A DRUM." Catrina studied her board. "Drum . . . drum . . . drum."

Not finding the pictograph, she set her bean to the side of her tabla.

"I, too, am without a drum," Life said.

The clang of metal on stone echoed through the space as a merchant lost his grip on the pole he was using to support his stand. Two of his fellow merchants rushed to his aid, and soon the stand was up and tightly bound. The three men worked together to set up the remaining stands.

Colorful tarps sheltered tables lined with fantastical alebrijes and ornaments made of flattened tin. There were bowls and vases, platters and plates of black clay; shirts and blouses shared a space with hand-embroidered bags; and everywhere there were baskets of fried crickets.

Big vats of tejate—a creamy drink made out of cacao beans and maize, and dating from prehistoric times—were being stirred with large molinillos. The beverage was served alongside tamales and tortillas, hot off sizzling griddles. Scattered strands of conversation mingled in the air, peppered with whispers and laughter.

An old woman hobbled on a cane to where Life and Death were seated. Draped in scarves and wrinkles, the woman extended her hand.

"For something to eat," she said.

Life placed some coins in her hand. Enough to feed her for more than a week.

The woman's eyes opened wide, overflowing with gratitude. "Gracias," she said, and made to leave.

"One moment," Catrina said. She touched the edge of the marigolds she had embroidered onto her skirts. The flowers bloomed in her hand, and she gave the bouquet to the old woman. The woman's face lit up as she slipped the coins into a small cloth bag tied around her wrist and clutched the flowers to her chest.

As she walked away, the woman gradually transformed. Her gray, knotted hair smoothed and looped itself into a dark braid around her head. The weight of decades seemed to lift off her shoulders, and she straightened her back. Her weathered skin became silky and bright.

But it was not youth that Catrina had given her—that was not hers to give. Catrina's gift was of a different kind.

"You are generous with beauty," Life told her, and Catrina nodded.

Although, to be precise, Catrina had not given the woman beauty, either. Rather, the woman's heart brimmed with the *joy* of beauty, and it was her full heart that transformed her. The gift would last until the marigolds withered. But by then the old woman would have had a day of many happy fortunes.

The merchant whom Life and Death had come to see began setting up his wares. He unfolded an old card table and draped a bright pink cloth over it. Carefully he laid out delicate chains of silver and gold, then shimmering pendants and elaborate charms. Even from a distance Catrina could admire the skillful designs.

The merchant's stand, slightly off balance and tented with a cheap plastic tarp, did not look like much. But that did not dull his reputation as a master jeweler, and his expertise was precisely why Life and Death were paying him a visit.

The friends were well aware of the implications of the Lotería. And it was their custom to deliver a gift to the pawn they subjected to the game.

The jeweler looked up as Life and Death approached his stand.

"Buenas noches," he said.

"Good evening," Life replied.

Catrina studied the various pendants and charms on the table.

"Can I help you find something in particular?" the merchant asked.

"We're looking for a gift," Life explained. "A token of our deepest appreciation."

Catrina nodded. "The recipient has brought us together."

"But at a great cost to herself," Life added.

"I see," the merchant said. "You need something truly special, then." He reached into his workbag and pulled out a stone.

It was an unassuming stone, blindingly white, smooth and polished to a gleam.

"White marble," the merchant said. "Black on the other side."

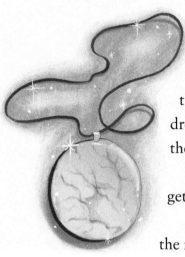

Catrina turned the pendant over. The smooth black disk caught the light from a nearby lantern, casting it onto one of the blossoms stitched on Catrina's dress. The petals opened to receive the light.

"How are the two sides held together?" Catrina asked.

"They're not. It's a single stone," the merchant replied.

"Remarkable!" Catrina turned the pendant over once again. A small bale had been attached to the top of the stone through which a silver chain was threaded.

The merchant's eyes smiled as he went on. "This piece is not quite finished, señora."

"Oh?" Catrina looked up.

"I may be skilled at making jewelry, but I am just a man. To complete this necklace requires the kind of magic that only nature can provide."

"I'm most intrigued," Catrina said.

The merchant leaned over. "Take this pendant to the big temple at Monte Albán. You must be there at the exact moment when the night meets the day. Hold the white side up to the moon and the black side to the rising sun."

"What will happen?"

The man grinned. "Then the gift will be finished."

"How clever," Life said.

The man inclined his head. "The idea came to me quite unexpectedly," he explained. "But I promise it works."

"It's perfect." Without waiting for the merchant to state a price, Life paid him the stone's true value— a bounty that would feed the man and his family for a year.

The merchant struggled to speak.

"Thank you." Catrina slipped the necklace into her purse.

"Did you hear what he said?" Life asked as they returned to their table.

"That the idea just came to him?"

"Exactly. Imagination."

Catrina smiled. "The idea may have come to him unexpectedly, but broad though his imagination may be, it was still inspired by *something*. It wasn't an arbitrary decision plucked out of thin air."

As she spoke, she plucked a petal off her crown and released it into the air. The petal folded into a rose-scented butterfly.

"You see, a person can never know what they don't know. Which is to say, there is a limit to what they can imagine—or reason, for that matter."

"And what they know is based on past experiences." Life sighed. "My dear, you are making it very difficult for me to win this debate."

Catrina laughed.

"But I'm not giving up just yet," Life added.

"I would hope not! After all, the game is not over."

"Not yet." Life flipped over the top card of the deck. "SALTANDO VA BUSCANDO, PERO NO VE NADA," he said.

"JUMPING, IT GOES SEARCHING," Catrina murmured as

she searched for the pictograph of the deer, "BUT IT SEES NOTHING."

She placed her frijole back on the table while Life placed a black bean on the image of a deer. "Three in a row." He pointed at his tabla. "It seems I'm finally making progress. At least in the game."

"And so it does," Catrina replied.

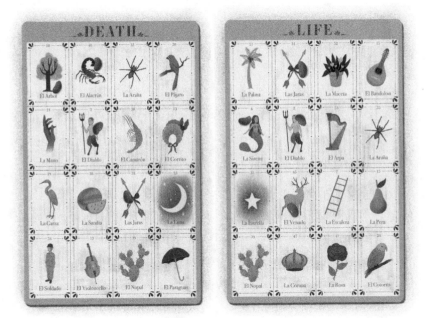

CHAPTER 20

"EL VENADO"

Clara tried in vain to push her way through the vines. Her hands were cut, raw and bloodied from the effort. But her determination numbed the pain. The thought of Esteban alone in this world made her relentless.

She resisted the urge to cry, instead hurling angry words at the impassable green wall.

"This place is absurd!" she yelled. "Grown-ups who kidnap children, and stupid birds that want unicorn horns, and nobody willing to help unless they get something in return, and—"

A sudden rustling of leaves momentarily startled her into silence.

"Who's there?" She turned around. Her labored

breath crowded out any other sounds, but still Clara sensed a shift in the air. She could feel it, if not see it—something was near.

Slowly Clara lowered herself to the ground, keeping her eyes trained straight ahead. She groped around for something she could use to defend herself. Her hand clasped a jagged rock, and she clutched it tightly. She kept her head low and her body still.

For a while, nothing happened. Perhaps it had been her imagination. But then a flash of white behind a mass of leaves caught her attention. She spotted a limb, an ear, a jet-black eye gazing at her unblinkingly.

Clara sucked in her breath. Whatever the creature was, it had her directly in its sight.

Breathe.

And yet it hadn't attacked. The creature had probably been staring at Clara the whole time she'd been searching for it, and it hadn't made a move.

It's afraid.

Clara rose from her crouch. The leaves rustled, and she saw the creature shift behind them.

"It's all right," she whispered. "I won't hurt you."

To prove her point, she dropped the rock. Startled, the creature shifted once more. But still it did not attack.

"It went this way!" A voice preceded a group of people who raced out from the jungle to her right.

The men wore pelts made of white fur and had leather belts around their waists. Daggers hung from their belts. They each carried a bow and a quiver of arrows. Leather bands encircled their heads, with colorful feathers festooning down over their stark white hair. The oldest in the group had the most feathers; the youngest—a boy no older than Esteban—had one.

"Oh, thank goodness," Clara cried. "Finally, someone who can help!"

The group froze. Each set of eyes turned toward her.

"Who are you?" the elder called. "What are you doing here?"

Clara walked toward them, but the elder put up one hand, and with the other he gripped his knife. "Stay there," he said.

Clara stopped. "I just need your help. It's my cousin. He was taken by a bad man, and they're on the other side of that hedge."

She pointed at the wall of vines behind her. "Please, I think he's in danger."

The elder frowned.

"Can you cut through some of these vines?" Clara asked, her words spilling out in a frenzied plea. "I only need a space big enough for me to get through."

"What can you give us?" the elder barked.

Clara jumped at the harshness in his voice. The

hunters closed ranks, gathering closer; a few placed their hands on their daggers. Clara took a step back.

"I—I—" she stammered. "I have nothing to give. I'm not from here, and I didn't know—"

"We have no use for you," the elder growled, and turned his back on her. The group began to move on.

"Wait!" Clara called after them. A wave of heat rose from her neck and spread across her face. "Maybe I can . . . draw you something."

A pause of less than a second was followed by laughter.

"What do you think we would do with a child's drawing?" one of the hunters said. His eyes danced with ridicule.

"Absurd!" another hunter scoffed. "Let's get out of here," he added.

"Papa," the youngest hunter spoke up. "She might know where the fawn went."

A fawn!

All at once the laughter ceased, and the hunters turned back to her.

"Do you?" The elder's voice was as sharp and cutting as his gaze.

Clara blinked at his intensity but forced herself to keep her eyes steady on him, to avoid giving away the fawn's location with an inadvertent glance.

His expression narrowed as he studied her. "If you tell us where the creature went, we'll help you."

Except that she'd pay with the fawn's life.

We must honor all living creatures. It is not our right to restrict anyone's freedom.

It felt so long ago that Chita had spoken those words to Esteban. At the time, they had seemed small and unimportant when they only related to a tiny spider. But they now took on a deeper meaning.

Whether she liked it or not, the fawn's life was not hers to give.

"Is there something else I can give you?" Clara asked. "Anything?"

"Enough of this, Father," a hunter said. "Let's go."

The elder gave a whistle, and as suddenly as the hunters had arrived, they were gone.

Clara didn't bother calling them back. She knew they wouldn't return. As she watched the group vanish through the trees, she felt doubly trapped: first by her insecurity with the bird, and now by her convictions.

CHAPTER 21

IN WHICH FEAR
IS ALSO A TRAP

"Thank you for not telling them where I was."

Startled, Clara turned. The baby deer had left its hiding place and now stood behind her. It was completely white, a bright beacon against the greens and reds and yellows surrounding them. Its large black eyes gazed at her openly. The fawn nuzzled against her hand. Clara could feel its heart racing when she stroked its alabaster fur.

"You're an easy target with fur so white," she said.

"I know," the fawn replied. Then it added, "I heard what you said about your cousin. The Kingdom of Las Pozas is a place you want to avoid."

"Why is that?" Clara asked.

The fawn bowed its head. "It's the home of El Diablo. He collects children."

Clara's hand froze in midair.

"What do you mean he 'collects children'? Why?"

"I don't know," the fawn said. "But he steals into your world, opening passageways wherever he sees heartbreak."

Clara's throat tightened as questions piled up, one on top of another.

The fawn went on. "The children he collects . . . They never return."

"*What?*" Clara turned back to the impassable wall of vines.

"There *is* a way in," the fawn said. "But it's dangerous."

Clara didn't even let the words sink in before she pleaded with the fawn. "You must show me!"

"First, we need to figure out what to trade," the fawn said.

"Trade? But I saved your life! Isn't that good enough?"

"I didn't ask for your help," the fawn replied. "It was given freely."

"But they would have killed you!" Clara cried.

The fawn nodded; a shiver rippled across its bright white fur. "And you would have contributed to my death. All acts have consequences."

Chita's words echoed in Clara's memory: *We always pay a price.*

"Well, shouldn't *good* deeds be rewarded, then?"

"Good deeds have great value," the fawn agreed. "And yours was no exception. Do you know the wall is enchanted?"

Clara looked at the vines that had impeded her passage. Of course! That explained why she had struggled so much.

"Even if you had traded my life with those hunters, they wouldn't have been able to cut through the vines. I would have perished and you would have gained nothing. As it is, I happen to know a way in that the hunters do not. So it's a good thing I'm alive."

Clara studied the fawn. It was impossible to know whether it was telling the truth.

"Your good deed is what will help you find a way into Las Pozas," the fawn continued. "*If* we can find something to trade."

Clara shook her head. "You heard me tell the hunters I don't have anything to trade."

"Actually, you do have something that could be quite useful to me."

"Anything!" Clara cried. "What can I give you?"

"Your help," the fawn replied.

"How?" Clara asked.

"As you said, I am an easy target, and it is almost impossible for me to hide once the hunters have me in their sights. I was lucky this time because you distracted them. However, I may not be so lucky the next time."

"But—but how can I help?"

"Give me your hair," the fawn replied.

"My hair?"

"The color of your hair."

Clara looked down at her long dark braids.

"I have no use for anything else," the fawn said. "I'm sorry."

Somewhere in the distance a bell began to toll.

"What is that?" Clara asked.

"It happens every day at this hour," the fawn explained. "It comes from Las Pozas. Five bells means the Mercado Rojo is open."

The bell tolled a second time.

"The Mercado Rojo?"

"The Red Market is a secret market, for people who

want to trade goods and services that are not part of your world."

A third bell rang.

"I don't understand," Clara said. "What kind of goods and services?"

"Charms and curses, fortune-telling and fortune-making, the sale of long-dead creatures . . . and children."

Clara's heart sped up as the fourth bell tolled.

"El Diablo trades children?" she asked. "To whom? Why?"

"There are many uses for children in our world—some more frightening than others."

"Like wh—"

The bell rang a fifth time, and it was followed by a terrific explosion, which Clara felt as a wave of pressure that crashed over her.

"Esteban!" she cried. Then she turned to the fawn.

This time she didn't hesitate.

"Fine," she said. "Take it. Just get me to the other side!"

The fawn nodded and began licking Clara's arm. A blush of color tinged its fur: faint and pale at first, then warming to a milky brown. As the fawn's pelt took on a darker hue, Clara's hair began to fade, first to a dusty brown, then a washed-out tan, and finally a stark and chalky white.

When it was all done, the fawn dipped its head. Clara gazed at the full spectrum of browns—chestnut, chocolate, coffee, cinnamon—swimming in its fur.

"Thank you," the fawn said.

Clara's braids fell limply over her shoulders. It was a small thing, she knew, but the loss made her feel cold, stripped of herself.

"And now you must move quickly," the fawn said.

Clara nodded. There was no time to indulge her sorrow. "Okay. Show me the way."

The fawn led Clara to the right, following the wall of vines.

"I've been this way already," she said. "There's no entrance."

"There is," the fawn said, "if you know where to look." They continued walking, eventually stopping at a segment of the vines that looked no different from any other. With its snout, the fawn indicated an almost imperceptible opening on the ground beneath the hedge.

"It's a tunnel," the fawn said. "It'll take you to the castle garden. The animals use it to forage for food."

"That's perfect," Clara replied. "Thank you!"

"A word of warning, though. The tunnel runs deep below the wall of the vines, but the vines still have a way of knowing when someone is traveling through it."

"How?"

"They sense fear." The fawn paused. "If you are not careful to keep your fear in check, they will find you."

The fawn didn't say what would happen if the vines found Clara. It simply added, "Good luck!" Then it sprinted off, leaving Clara alone, staring into the mouth of the tunnel.

They sense fear.

She took a deep breath.

"I'm not afraid," she whispered, each word trembling as it fell to the ground.

The tunnel entrance was small, and she had to crawl on her hands and knees, sucking in her breath, to squeeze through.

As the tunnel sloped downward, the soil became damper, the light became dimmer, and Clara's nerves echoed ever louder in her ears. Slimy things squirmed under her hands, and bits of earth crumbled onto her head. The air was stale and warm, and the farther she went, the more suffocating it became.

Clara stopped to catch her breath.

Before her there was only darkness; behind her, a pinpoint of light. It occurred to her that the fawn may have tricked her, that this tunnel might lead nowhere, and that by the time she figured it out, the deer would be long gone . . . and she would be trapped under-ground.

I can't do this.

She scooted backward, letting her feet guide her toward the entrance. Panic lodged itself in her throat. Gulping down breaths of stale air, she forced herself to move as quickly as she could.

And then something crumbled in the space behind her. She heard it clearly, the earth shifting. Before she could figure out what it was or what to do, a cold finger touched her ankle.

Clara gasped, and her heart constricted inside her chest. A second finger made contact with her skin, and a strangled cry escaped her throat. But the cry prompted her to action. She raced forward, crawling as fast as she could. Needles of pain shot up her arms as dirt and small stones lodged into the cuts on her palms.

Her breath came fast, almost drowning out the sound of the earth crumbling: behind her, beneath her, over her head. It was as if the tunnel was preparing to collapse. The notion of all that dirt above her stole her breath, but she pushed away the thought and focused instead on just moving.

As the tunnel leveled off, Clara found it easier to gain speed. But she wasn't fast enough to stop the cold tendrils reaching for her arms and legs. One looped itself around her right foot and yanked her back, hard.

Clara dug her fingers into the ground; dirt jammed up under her fingernails. With her free foot, she kicked at the cold thing pulling her back. It only tightened its grip.

She planted her left foot on the ground and firmly pushed herself forward, using her elbows for leverage. Her right foot felt numb as the tightness around her ankle increased. She pushed onward, fighting for every inch of progress. But the pressure around her foot intensified and a dull pain pulsed up her leg.

A second tendril crawled up her left foot, and before she could stop it, the thing wrapped itself around her leg, completely immobilizing her.

A sob rose in Clara's throat as she realized that the fawn's warning had come to pass: the vines had been alerted to her fear. They had found her, and they *were* dangerous. The grinding of earth all along the tunnel made it clear that more vines were swiftly making their way toward her.

"Esteban!" she called out in the darkness.

Her voice was swallowed up by the many layers of sediment between Clara and her cousin, who at that moment happened to be standing directly above her, realizing that maybe it hadn't been such a good idea to follow the man in red.

CHAPTER 22

IN WHICH ESTEBAN
REGRETS HIS DECISION

The man had come out of nowhere, a kind smile on his face, and eyes that reminded Esteban of his father ("honest eyes," his mother always said).

"Hey, little fellow." The man had knelt on the ground, surely ruining his elegant pants. His jacket was also very fancy and shiny and red. Something shuffled inside his breast pocket, and the small head of a dragon poked out, followed quickly by a second tiny head. The man in red put a hand over his pocket and whispered words under his breath. The heads dropped out of sight, and the shuffling stopped.

"Are you okay?" the man asked Esteban.

"I—I think I'm lost," Esteban replied.

The man nodded.

"I don't know how I got here." Esteban looked around. "I thought I heard my mother. . . ."

His sentence fell off into silence, and his eyes welled with tears.

"You mustn't cry," the man said. He put a hand on Esteban's shoulder. "I have it on good authority that your mother is, in fact, nearby."

"She is?" Esteban lit up.

"Indeed, she is. And she's eager to see you."

The man stood and brushed the dirt off his pants. He held a hand out to Esteban. "Shall we go meet her?"

"Yes, oh, please!"

Anticipation coursed through Esteban as he took the man's hand.

"You must miss her," the man said.

"I do. So much!"

As they walked, Esteban told the man all about Chita, and the man told him about the beautiful pink castle where he lived.

"Is Mami in the castle?"

"Yes," the man said. "She's been waiting for you. Now come, it's just up ahead."

They passed by a large hedge of thickly entangled vines, and for a moment Esteban thought he'd heard Clara's voice.

He turned.

"There are dangerous things beyond that hedge," the man whispered in his ear. "We must hurry."

Esteban followed the man, and they crossed through an enormous ring made of stone and onto a smooth platform at the edge of a cliff, overlooking the tops of trees.

Thin steps descended from the platform, seemingly floating in midair. They led to a second platform, which was flanked by two enormous stone blossoms. Steps wrapped around the stem of each flower in a downward spiral that disappeared into the treetops.

"This way." The man led Esteban down the spiral stairs. As they descended, more of the kingdom revealed itself.

It was unlike anything Esteban had ever seen.

Tall metal structures rose like stalks of rusted seaweed; impossibly thin bridges crisscrossed the trees; tapered stone columns held giant bowls overflowing with flowering vines.

There were tall constructions with walls made of interconnected ovals through which the jungle had woven itself, creating an interlacing tapestry of green and stone. Others had slender walls reaching up to the sky with no roof. Still others had walls that rose and then curved outward like petals on a blossom.

A waterfall roared down the side of the cliff into a pool of clear water that branched off into dozens of canals. The canals snaked along the jungle floor toward fountains carved in the shape of mermaids or fish or outstretched hands with fingers reaching upward.

The ground was paved with stones interspersed with moss. A path made of colorful pieces of glass stood out among the stones, and it was this path that Esteban and the man in red followed.

They passed the frame of a building with intricately carved pillars on thin platforms and steps leading up and into thin air. A lattice of arches rose beside them like waves frozen in stone.

Esteban marveled at the wonders unfolding before him. It didn't surprise him that his mother would be in a place like this.

The man in red stopped before a grand and imposing entrance; a large metal door was set into the stone, framed by a tangle of what appeared to be vines of solid gold.

"Come." The man beckoned.

From his jacket, he pulled out a skeleton key, ancient and rusted. He put the key in the keyhole and turned it once.

Esteban hadn't noticed how loud the jungle was

until it fell silent with the turning of the key. A shiver raced down his back; goose bumps flooded his skin.

With a loud creak, the door opened into a dark cave within the cliff.

"Hurry!" The man motioned for Esteban to follow him. Somewhere in the jungle a bell rang.

Esteban stopped. "Do you hear that?"

"Yes," the man said. "We must be behind this door before the final bell tolls." He placed a hand on Esteban's shoulder, gently nudging him forward.

The bell rang a second time.

"Is my mother in here?" Esteban asked, peering into the cave.

The man nodded. "Yes, yes." But his words were too quick, and his manner gave Esteban pause. He lingered on the threshold.

The bell rang a third time.

"Come on now," the man in red urged.

"Mami?" Esteban called into the cave. The word bounced back at him. He looked at the man. "She's not here."

The bell rang a fourth time.

A shadow fell across the face of the man in red. But it was gone as quickly as it came. The next moment, he was smiling.

"Of course she's here." His long fingers wrapped around Esteban's arm. With a hard yank, he pulled Esteban through the door and into the cave.

Esteban stumbled but caught himself before he fell. Meanwhile, the man in red slammed the large metal door shut and locked it with his ancient key.

In the darkness that surrounded him, Esteban heard the faint sound of the bell tolling a fifth time, followed by a muffled bang against the door. "What was—" But before he could finish his question, the walls of the cave began to pulse with light. At first the light was dim and hardly noticeable, but with every passing second it intensified, until the walls glowed brightly.

"Whoa!" Esteban ran his hand over the smooth pink crystal surface.

"Welcome to my home." The man in red grinned. Then he turned the key in the lock of the metal door through which they had just entered. The door opened onto the very same place as before, but the scene was entirely different. It was as if the key had removed a veil shielding a magic kingdom hidden in the jungle.

What had appeared to be overgrown ruins was now a shining citadel made of pink granite, with colored windows that glittered in the sunshine and staircases leading to second and third and fourth floors, all with walls intact and engraved with gems making intricate patterns. Water sparkled from countless crystal fountains, and large colorful umbrellas created a bright canopy for the dozens of people who were milling around, talking gaily and laughing.

Ladies wore flowing gowns of shimmering silk embroidered with gold and silver threads. Flowers and feathers were woven into their hair. Men wore suits of deep green, blue, and purple hues, with flowers tucked into their lapels or on the bands of their hats. Peacocks moved among them, dragging their long iridescent feathers along the ground.

The man in red stepped out of the cave, and Esteban followed him. The crowd turned toward the man in red and bowed.

"Welcome, friends!" the man called out. He kept a hand firmly on Esteban's shoulder. "El Mercado Rojo is now open!"

Esteban had never heard of the Red Market, but it was clearly an important event for the people gathered around. A cheer burst from the crowd, and a man began pounding on a large drum. With every beat of the drum, sparks filled the air, rippling outward from the instrument.

Behind him, another musician played a wooden flute. A woman followed next, with a mandolin. There were guitars and bells, a harp on golden wheels. Each instrument added its own texture to the air, enveloping the spectators and drawing them forward.

Esteban raised his hand, feeling the harmonies course through his fingertips and down to his bones.

The people gathered in a joyous line behind the musicians, dancing and singing. They clapped in unison as they wound around gleaming towers of metal roses, under curtains of sweet-scented flowers, and over small gem-encrusted bridges, beneath which clear water reflected all the colors of this glorious symphony.

Their merriment was contagious, and Esteban took a step to follow them. A firm hand stopped him in his tracks. The man in red stood beside him, gazing out at the ambling crowd.

"You will go to the Mercado Rojo later," he said. "First, it's time to get you ready." The man turned his gaze toward Esteban. A hunger glinted in his eyes, similar to what Esteban often saw in the eyes of the stray dogs near his home.

"Ready for what?" Esteban asked.

The man smiled. "To see your mother, of course."

A growing sense of unease had settled into Esteban's stomach. He recognized it as a premonition.

"Is she far?" he asked.

"Not far at all." The man turned and walked away from the gaily dancing crowd. His shoes clicked sharply on the path of polished pink stone, like a clock tick-tick-ticking or a boy's heart beat-beat-beating faster with every passing moment.

The jungle grew increasingly silent as they followed the path, until Esteban could hear only his breath and the rhythmic clicking of shoes.

Sculpted snakes rose alongside them, their jaws open, their fangs tipped in silver. Large bowls rested atop slender stalks of stone, gathering water and birds. Everywhere there were palms, ferns, crawling vines, and flowers dripping from branches.

The man in red led Esteban over a bridge made of a thin sheet of glass. Tall and perfectly even tree trunks, stripped of leaves and branches, stood in a dense row along the bridge, creating a makeshift wall. Below the bridge, jewel-toned fish swam in a pool of clear water.

At the end of the bridge, steps led down to a garden enclosed by tall walls covered in leaves. Unlike the jungle, wild and untamed, the garden was perfectly trimmed and orderly.

Along the sides of the garden, lush fruit trees in tidy rows provided shade for the white benches interspersed beneath their branches. Directly in front of Esteban, hundreds of tulips made an intricate geometric design. Lavender bushes framed the tulips, with bees swarming dizzyingly among the stalks.

The garden stood at the base of a pink castle. But this was no ordinary castle. Slender pillars held up equally thin ceilings, which in turn supported more pillars holding up more ceilings holding up more pillars, and so on, as high as Esteban could see. The structure resembled a house of cards.

"Is this where you live?" Esteban asked.

The man in red nodded.

"And my mother is here, too?"

"You'll see her soon enough," the man replied, but Esteban couldn't see any people anywhere, and he was starting to doubt that this man actually knew where his mother was.

"Now come," the man said.

"I—I want to see my mother *first*," Esteban said. His stomach tightened.

The man stopped but did not turn around.

"You said you'd take me to see her," Esteban added.

A hush fell upon them, and all that Esteban could hear was a rustling sound from the vine-covered wall along the garden's edge. A chill crawled across his body.

"Look." The man turned abruptly. "Why don't you just come with me and we'll sort this all out."

"You don't know where she is, do you?" Esteban took a step backward. The rustling around him grew louder, more active.

The man in red sighed.

"I want to go back." Esteban fought a wave of nausea. "To my house."

The place was a maze, but he was sure he could find his way.

"I'm sorry," said the man. "I truly am. But that's no longer possible."

Esteban's next step was cut short by a sharp pain in his stomach that made him double over. The strength of his premonition left him gasping for air.

The wall around the garden began to expand, closing off the entrance.

"No!" Esteban cried, and he ran toward the narrowing gap the vines were quickly sealing. He would have made it, he would have reached the exit, except that he tripped on his shoelace, which—in his haste to find his mother when he crawled out of his window so many lifetimes ago—he had forgotten to tie.

With a heavy thud, Esteban crashed to the ground, skinning his hands and knees. The air in his lungs momentarily fled his body, sending him into a breathless panic.

He sucked in air, breath after breath, fighting back his pain. And then he heard his name being called. It was so very faint and so far away he was certain it was just wishful thinking.

Still, he called out in response. "Clara?"

The word fell to the ground, sinking through grass and soil until it reached his cousin, bound tightly in a mesh of creepers far below him.

CHAPTER 23

IN WHICH LIFE AND DEATH VISIT MONTE ALBÁN, AND NATURE MAKES JEWELRY

Six miles west of the city center, Life and Death sat in the back of a taxi winding its way up a mountain. The narrow road hardly seemed big enough for one small car, let alone the two lanes of traffic it usually carried. Fortunately, at that hour the road was empty. The friends were on a tight schedule, and it would be best if Catrina didn't have new souls to tend to before they completed their task.

"I told you, señora," the cabdriver said as he pulled into the parking lot near the top of the mountain. "It's closed."

"That's quite all right," Catrina replied, and she paid the man handsomely. "This is all we needed."

Of course, they didn't need to take the taxi at all.

A simple snap of the fingers would have transported them to their destination. But Life and Death enjoyed these rare moments when they got to pretend they were human.

They climbed out of the taxi and bid the driver farewell, watching until the car's taillights faded into the darkness before turning toward the entrance of Monte Albán.

The cabdriver had not lied. The vast pre-Columbian archaeological site was empty at this hour, save for the ghosts of the ancient priests and nobles who had occupied the area since 500 BC. The terraces, temples, pyramids, and artificial mounds that made up Monte Albán had been carved directly into the mountain and inhabited by a succession of ancient peoples: first the Olmec, then the Zapotec, and finally the Mixtec.

Life and Death climbed to the top of the tallest pyramid and took a seat on the stone ledge. From their perch, they watched over all of Oaxaca City, fast asleep beneath them.

The sky was beginning to show signs of dawn: gilded streaks of coral and amber cutting through the deep blue of night. The rising sun kissed the windows and bells in the city below, creating squares of light all across town. A flock of birds rose to greet the sun, their black shadows crossing over from night to day.

Catrina removed the black-and-white pendant from her purse. She held the white side toward the moon and the black side toward the sun. A ray of sunlight broke away and reached for the pendant. As it did, the moon reached out as well. Both made contact at the very same moment—a flash of gold and silver.

Catrina lowered the pendant, admiring the smattering of silver dots that now glittered on the white side and the flecks of gold embedded on the black side. She handed it to Life.

"And did you notice?" he said. "The white side is smooth and cool to the touch. The black side seems to be radiating heat."

"A truly remarkable gift," Catrina said.

"That it is." Life returned the pendant to Catrina, and the two friends descended the steep steps of the pyramid arm in arm. They took their time, ambling in silence across the vast lawn with all its tombs and pyramids as the ancestral ghosts vanished in the growing light.

Soon the area would be swarming with tourists, but at that moment, as they made their way to a wooden table set up for picnics, it was a peaceful sanctuary for the two friends and a friendly cat, which dropped a mouse at Life's feet. The mouse was not quite dead, and Life gently pressed a finger upon its quivering fur. With a squeak, the mouse jumped and scampered away.

Before the cat could follow in pursuit, Life ran his fingers along the cat's fur.

"It was a generous gift," he told the cat, now purring contentedly. "Thank you."

Catrina gazed into the small silver mirror displaying Clara's unfolding fate.

"The girl has surprised me," she admitted. "I did not anticipate her courage."

"I don't think she anticipated it, either," Life replied. He pulled out the tablas and the cards.

"I suppose we all need help seeing the truth within us." Catrina smiled. "Even if that help comes in painful ways."

"Indeed," Life agreed.

A bird flitted over to the table. The cat made a leap for it, and the bird fled to Catrina's shoulder. Before it could utter a chirp, Catrina pressed a bony finger on its quivering feathers, and the bird unraveled into many colorful threads that then embroidered themselves onto the sleeve of her dress. An exact replica of the little bird now perched on a cluster of stitched roses.

"Shall we continue?" Life asked.

Catrina nodded, and Life flipped the top card from

the Lotería deck. "AL VER A LA VERDE RANA, QUÉ BRINCO PEGÓ TU HERMANA."

"WHAT A JUMP YOUR SISTER GAVE WHEN SHE SAW THE GREEN FROG." Catrina shook her head. "There is no frog on my tabla."

"Or mine," Life replied.

He uttered the next riddle: "EL QUE POR LA BOCA MUERE, AUNQUE MUDO FUERE."

"THE ONE WHO DIES BY ITS MOUTH, EVEN IF IT CANNOT SPEAK. A reference to the fish."

A petal landed on Catrina's tabla as she bent her head over it, looking for the fish. She plucked the petal off the board and gave it to the wind. "Alas, no fish." She peered over at Life's tabla. "You?"

Life shook his head and flipped over a third card. "ROSITA, ROSAURA, VEN QUE TE QUIERO AHORA."

"ROSITA, ROSAURA, COME BECAUSE I WANT YOU NOW," Catrina repeated. "The rose!"

As she spoke the word, a new rose bloomed on her crown.

"Finally!" Life placed a black bean on the image of a blood-red rose.

"And so the story resumes," Catrina declared.

CHAPTER 24

"LA ROSA"

A raccoon was in the tunnel on his way back from the garden when he felt the ground moving around him. Thinking he was being punished for his act of thievery, he dropped the food he'd filched and scurried away. But he didn't get far, for there was a tangle of vines blocking his passage. A creature appeared to be caught up in it. Muffled cries came from the vines, and the raccoon inched closer to inspect the creature.

A hand reached for the raccoon, who instantly pulled back.

"Wait!" a voice called out. "Please help me."

Unfortunately, it was not in this raccoon's nature

to be helpful. Indeed, he was rather greedy, selfish, and sometimes quite mean. As soon as he realized that the rumble of dirt wasn't a threat, he retreated and recovered his bounty. From a distance he watched as Clara struggled to disentangle herself. Her efforts were in vain, as the vines gripped her tight. Eventually, she had to stop to catch her breath. By then, the raccoon was losing his patience: he was hungry and eager to get home.

Clutching his food with one paw, the raccoon approached Clara, sniffing for a way around her.

"Hey," Clara called out again, reaching toward him, perhaps in an effort to steal his food.

Fearful of the girl's intentions, the raccoon clutched the food tighter and dug into the dirt by her feet. It was slow going, as he refused to release his bounty, but eventually he managed to carve a passage in the wall alongside the girl. The whole time, she struggled and continued to call for help. However, the raccoon had other plans, and he focused entirely on his task.

As the passage grew larger, the raccoon became more excited and dug faster, until he cleared a space just wide enough for his slender body to squeeze past—that is, had he been willing to leave the food behind. But the greedy raccoon was not willing to consider that.

In his eagerness to expand the hole, he had alerted the vines to a new intruder. The vines, which did not discriminate among intruders, shifted their focus to him and loosened their hold on Clara.

When the raccoon felt the first vine gripping his hind leg, he tried to pull away with a jerk, but that only made the vine cling to him tighter. He responded by clutching the food even more greedily and digging with a fiercer determination.

Other vines released Clara's body and moved to ensnare the greedy creature. As they did, Clara was able to slither out of the tangle. One vine wrapped itself around the raccoon's leg, and another quickly took hold of his body. By then, Clara had escaped her trap completely, which was now nothing more than a loose coil slithering toward the new captive.

Clara was nearly free when the raccoon whimpered. But she had wasted so much time already and did not want to get caught in the netting again.

"Help me!" the raccoon cried out. "Please."

Clara stopped, and without giving herself time to change her mind, she turned back for the trapped animal.

She thrust her hands into the tangle of vines and pulled with all her might, making an opening wide enough for the raccoon to squeeze through.

"Run!" she called as the vines writhed in her hands, like snakes coming to life. "Leave the food!"

But the selfish creature refused to let go of his stash, and he couldn't fit through the gap with such a large bundle.

"Make it bigger!" he cried as the vines wound their way around Clara's wrist.

"I'm sorry!" She swatted at the vines, yanking her arms away from their grip, then turned and fled from their onslaught. The telltale shifting of earth at her feet left no doubt in her mind that the vines were in hot pursuit, but the exit was close. With a final push, she flung herself out into the light, landing with a crash in a patch of brambles.

Scrambling to get away from the tunnel as quickly as possible, she pushed herself deeper into the brambles. There was no need: the vines had long since retreated to deal with the raccoon, who had chosen to live by greed and, in so doing, sealed his fate.

Clara would never know it, but the fawn's statement about good deeds having their own value had proved true once more. Had Clara not gone back to help the raccoon and spent those extra seconds trying to persuade him to forgo his food, she would have exited the tunnel right at the moment the man in red approached Esteban, lying on the ground not two feet away.

"Come now," she would have heard the man in red say, not unkindly. "The king awaits, and with him your mother."

And then Esteban would have turned and seen Clara. And the man in red would have seen her, too. Had that all happened, it would have made for a very different story. As it was, the man in red helped Esteban to his feet, brushed the dirt off the boy's clothes, and handed him a treat wrapped in shiny tinfoil.

"Eat this," he said. "It'll make you feel better."

Esteban unwrapped the foil to find a small polvorón tucked inside it; the crumbly sugar-dusted cookie was his mother's favorite. Without a second thought, he popped it into his mouth. As the cookie dissolved on his tongue, it seemed to take with it all of Esteban's worries and concerns.

A smile crawled across the face of the man in red. "Shall we?"

The boy didn't hesitate and gladly accepted the devil's hand, following him up to the pink castle.

But Clara missed all of that. Instead, she was lying in a heap among the briars, struggling to catch her breath as her eyes adjusted to the light.

A massive structure of pink and crumbling stone rose high above the trees. Where Esteban had seen a perfectly trimmed and orderly garden, Clara saw a wild disarray of once tended-to plants now being overrun by the jungle.

Faded benches lined the garden, and broken bird feeders hung from trees. An old basket nearby bulged with pears, brown and rotting. A pair of rusted shears caught the light.

Clara peeked through the bushes, expecting to see people walking around, but there was no one. She crawled out of her spot, keeping low to the ground and in the shadows. The thorns pulled at her hair and scratched her skin. She stifled a cry.

Once free of the brambles, she pressed her back to the vine-covered wall that encircled the garden and listened for voices. There were only birds and the distant trickle of water.

Clara inched toward the castle, stopping every now and then to listen.

"What are you doing?"

The voice was quiet, only a murmur, but it made Clara freeze in her tracks. Slowly she looked around for the source of the words.

I must be imagining things. She took a moment to steady her heart and catch a few breaths.

"Why are you here?" The voice spoke once more.

And once again Clara looked around but saw nothing. "Where are you?" she whispered.

"Up here," the voice replied.

Clara squinted into the sky. A cluster of roses rustled overhead, though there was no wind to move them.

Clara stood and examined the roses more closely.

"That's right," the voice said, and one of the blooms quivered. "You found me!" Then it added, "What are you doing here?"

"I'm looking for my cousin," Clara replied. "I think he might be here. . . ." She looked around. "Somewhere."

"A young boy?" the rose asked. "Looking for his mother?"

"Yes!" Clara gasped. "That's him. Did you see him?"

"I did," the rose replied. "But he's not yours to take. He belongs to El Diablo now."

"No," Clara said. "That man *took* Esteban! He stole him right out of his bed."

The rose giggled, and it seemed to Clara that the whole bush shared in the laughter.

"*Shhh!*" Clara begged.

The bush fell silent.

"El Diablo doesn't take people. They follow him," the rose explained. "There's a difference."

"Well . . . El Diablo tricked Esteban into following him," Clara replied.

"Maybe," the rose said. "But the boy walked in here all on his own. It was his choice. I saw him."

It was pointless to argue with a flower, and Clara was wasting valuable time. "Look, I just want to get my cousin back. Do you know where he is?"

"You'll never be able to rescue him," the rose said.

"Why not?"

"You're just a kid."

A renewed wave of laughter swept through the roses.

"You're no match for El Diablo."

Doubt slid its talons into Clara, attempting to get a firm grip. Of course, it was true: she *was* just a kid, and this magical world was wholly unfamiliar to her. It was clear El Diablo ruled here, and who knew what forces he had on his side.

And yet . . .

I've made it this far.

Despite all odds, Clara had managed to follow Esteban through a cactus and across an unfamiliar kingdom, all the way to this castle. She was not about to give up now.

"Please just tell me where he is," she said.

"What will you give me in return?"

"What do you want?"

"Those shears," the rose growled. Clara turned her gaze toward the basket heaped with pears and the rusty scissors. "Throw them over the wall!"

Clara scanned the garden to make sure nobody was watching and then sprinted to the basket. Up close, the pears looked as if they were made of glass imbedded with swirls of yellow and green. Her hands wrapped around the scissors, and she ran back to the wall of roses.

The flowers rustled anxiously, their petals fluttering frantically in the nonexistent breeze.

"Throw them over the wall!" the rose cried again.

Clara hurled the shears over the wall and heard them catch on a tangle of vegetation on the other side.

The flowers cheered, and a heady perfume wafted into the air.

"Okay, I did what you wanted. Now, where is he?" Clara demanded.

"He's in the castle," the rose replied.

Clara looked at the pink structure, held up precariously by crumbling pillars and slanting floors. "There's nobody there. It's empty."

"Ha! *That* is a trick. To keep people like you away."

Clara frowned. "How do I get in, then?"

"You have to be escorted in. As a guest," the rose told her, "or a prisoner."

"But how do I—"

Before she could finish her question, the blossoms on the wall erupted into a cacophony of wailing and screeching. Clara dropped to her knees and covered her ears.

Instantly, a swarm of guards spilled out of the castle and raced toward her, surrounding her in a matter of seconds.

One of the guards grabbed Clara and yanked her to her feet.

"You're welcome!" the rose called after her.

CHAPTER 25

IN WHICH ESTEBAN
ENTERS THE CASTLE

Esteban climbed the grand staircase leading to the castle entrance. Long ribbons of color flew from flag posts atop the castle, and flags waved proudly on twin poles flanking the entrance. The door was inlaid with tiny pieces of wood intricately arranged to form the spiral of a conch.

A guard bowed in greeting as the man in red led Esteban through the foyer and into a great hall.

The chamber they entered was circular, with walls that seemed to vanish into the sky. Glittering sunlight spilled into the room, and birds chased each other in and out of the angled shafts of light. A fresh breeze swept through, trailing the scent of jasmine.

A ramp with a gleaming silver railing wound upward

along the wall in an ever-rising spiral. People ambled along the ramp, talking and laughing, strolling in and out of rooms with different-colored doors. In the center of the chamber, a silver fountain bubbled directly out of the ground. It fed into three canals, which streamed into three separate wings of the castle. Music drifted from one of the wings, and it was toward the music that the man in red led Esteban.

"Where are we going?" the boy asked.

"To your room," the man replied.

A faint echo of Esteban's premonition pulsed inside his body, clamoring for attention. But his senses were dulled from a combination of the awe he felt at the marvels before him and the aftereffects of the crumbly cookie, making him dizzy and very sleepy. Snippets of his mother's song called to him from somewhere not too distant.

He followed the man in red along the canal that led to the left and under an archway leading to a second large hall, circular and sunny like the first, only smaller. The silver water burbled cheerfully alongside them, eventually feeding into a fountain in the center of the room.

Gathered around the fountain was a trio of musicians: a harpist, a cellist, and a flautist. As they played, their notes had an odd effect on the water, making it undulate and form whirlpools that turned into fantastical shapes.

An animal with an *S*-shaped neck and long slender legs sprung from the water. Strong wings spread out on either side of its body, and the bird took flight. As the music continued, more and more water birds rose into the air.

"Herons," the man in red explained. Esteban watched the birds, catching the rays of sun on their wings and casting diamonds of water at his feet. The herons danced until the music ended, and then they simply vanished, leaving behind a spray of rainbow drops.

"Bravo!" The man in red clapped when the trio finished their performance. "Bravo!"

The three musicians bowed, then took up their instruments once more. Esteban turned his gaze to the water in anticipation of the next performance, but the man put his hand on Esteban's shoulder and led him away.

"Come," he said. "We must get you ready."

Esteban nodded dreamily, vaguely aware of the ache in his belly. He followed the man up the sloping path along the wall, all the while running his hand along the silky-smooth silver banister. The friction created a sound, a single note that reverberated throughout the chamber.

On their way, they passed dozens of people. All bowed or curtsied to the man in red, but nobody gave Esteban a second glance.

"Here we are," the man said, abruptly stopping at a bright yellow door. He took a key from his jacket pocket. It was a long metal cylinder with a trefoil at one end. It fit smoothly into a round keyhole next to the door. With one quick turn of the key, the door vanished.

The room was sunny and bright yellow. A bed was piled high with cushions and soft blankets. Shelves held different-shaped jars of colorful liquids. The floor was carpeted in a plush rug that appeared to be made of fur. A wooden chest sat open, overflowing with toys, but Esteban's attention was quickly drawn to a slick black remote-controlled car on the desk.

"Yes," the man said. "I thought you'd like that."

He looked at his watch. "Now, we don't have much time. The Mercado Rojo is already open, and the king will be arriving shortly. He is expecting you at five o'clock, not a moment later. Is that clear?"

"Me?" Esteban asked. "Why is he expecting me?"

The man's smile spread even as his eyes hardened.

"The king loves children, but he cannot have his own. So I help him by finding children who are sad and lonely and need new homes. The king's castle is full of wonders and toys and everything you could ever want to eat."

"And my mother?"

"Yes, yes. Of course," the man replied. "Now, the next few hours are yours to spend as you choose. At three o'clock food will be brought to you and you will be cleaned and dressed. Do you understand?"

Esteban nodded.

Swiftly the man turned and walked toward the door. Without a glance back at Esteban, he stepped out of the room. As soon as he did, the yellow door reappeared behind him. There was no doorknob, no keyhole, no way out.

There was no question: Esteban was trapped.

He turned and looked around the small room. The calm he'd felt earlier was beginning to dissipate, and Esteban felt unsettled. The dull ache in his stomach grew into a cramp that he recognized as trouble. Doubt rose within him.

Something—a lot of things—didn't make sense. For instance, his mother's song had seemed so close, and yet she was nowhere to be seen. And who was this king, anyway? Esteban had never heard of him. And why was his mother with him? Why hadn't she told Esteban she'd be coming here?

The man in red seemed friendly enough, but Esteban couldn't ignore the feeling that he was hiding something important.

And why did he have to lock the door?

Esteban's doubts multiplied. Had he been tricked?

As the thought put down roots, his stomach cramped, splintering into shards of pain. Tears clouded his vision.

It was at that moment that a small box on one of the pillows caught his attention. Nestled inside the box were more small polvorones. Esteban eagerly reached for one of the cookies.

It melted on his tongue almost instantly. As it made its way into his bloodstream, it warmed him up and dulled his growing apprehension.

A second cookie flushed away his sorrow. The third and fourth cookies were simply an indulgence. After he'd gobbled them up, Esteban was more than happy to explore his surroundings.

He approached the wall of jars, taking down the

closest: a vial with a silky pink liquid that swirled in ribbons. He uncorked the bottle, and the liquid rose like a gas, then playfully wrapped around his arm. He waved his arm, and the pink dispersed into a million tiny drops. A second jar held a blue-gray smoke that slipped out onto his palm and formed a tight silver ball. An orange-yellow liquid exited another bottle as soon as he uncorked it and zipped under the door before he could catch it.

Esteban turned to the toys and his new remote-controlled car. The only evidence of his previous sorrow was a thin line of salt on his cheek where his tears no longer flowed.

CHAPTER 26

IN WHICH CLARA
ENTERS THE CASTLE

lara was dragged up the grand staircase to the castle entrance. The moment she reached the top step, the pink stone structure transformed before her eyes.

Where before there had been empty rooms yawning into the jungle, now there were walls of cold dark stone dripping with black water and slime. Tattered squares of cloth whipped in the wind on flag posts atop the castle and from twin poles flanking the entrance. The door was heavy iron, covered in sharp rusted spikes. A guard stood sentry at the door. He didn't even so much as glance at Clara as she was led through the foyer into the great hall.

The chamber they entered was circular, with walls

towering up into darkness. Cold daggers of artificial light cut through the air, and shadows raced between them. A heavy fog lingered at her feet, carrying the stench of decay.

An upward-sloping path pushed up against the wall as it wound its way past dark openings lined with steel bars. Guards were stationed at various points along the rising path.

An opening on the ground in the center of the chamber boiled with black water, oozing into three canals that led into different wings of the castle. Moans and whimpers mingled with the incessant dripping of water, and the wind whispered warnings as it raced through the catacombs of stone.

"Where are you taking me?" Clara cried. Her anger at the rose's betrayal burned through her veins and gave her a strength she didn't know she had. But the guards were stronger, and they held her in a tight grip.

In silence they pushed her forward, following the black canal to the right and beneath a cracked archway to a second chamber, identical to the first but smaller. Something heavy shuffled in the darkness, chains rattling across the cold stone. A shiver ran down Clara's back as she considered her options.

Fleeing was out of the question. Two guards held her fast, and more kept watch. She wouldn't get far. Even if she did manage to slip free of them, escape seemed unlikely. This place was obviously a fortress.

Persuasion might work, if she could get any of the guards to talk to her. But what could she say? They didn't have any decision-making power; they were just following orders. No, she needed to talk to whoever was in charge.

"I want to see the man in red," she said. "El Diablo."

The guards continued to ignore her.

"Did you hear me?" she yelled. Her words echoed back at her full force. And something howled. "I want to talk to El Diablo!"

The guards moved in lockstep, dragging Clara between them up the sloping ramp that ran along the chamber wall. She dug her heels, trying to slow their progress. But the floor was slippery and gave her no traction.

Before she could come up with a plan, they stopped at a door made of rusted metal bars. One guard took a key out of his pocket. It was a long metal cylinder with a triangle at one end. The cylinder fit smoothly into the round keyhole, and when the guard turned the key, the door opened, revealing a pitch-black cave.

Clara was shoved into the darkness. Tripping on something, she fell onto the slick and slimy floor. Despite the sudden jolt of pain that coursed up her arms and legs, she quickly scrambled to her feet. But by the time she turned around, the guards were gone, leaving her imprisoned behind thick metal bars.

"Hey!" Clara called. "Come back!" Her voice bounced off the walls in a series of echoes.

But nobody came back.

She was stuck in a dark cave in a sinister castle hidden within a magical jungle in a kingdom that was completely unknown. And she was all alone.

If ever there was a time for hopelessness, this was it.

CHAPTER 27

IN WHICH LOVE ENTERS THE PICTURE

Life and Death had just made their way down the winding road that led from Monte Albán into the city when the sound of merriment caught up with them.

"A calenda!" Catrina smiled. "A splendid way to spend our last day. Let's meet up with it."

"Very well," Life said. "Which way shall we go?" The companions were at a crossroads.

"You choose," Catrina replied, a hint of laughter in her voice.

"Ha! A test of free will. I see. But how to choose?" Life turned to Catrina. "Tell me, you who have known me for so very long, what does my past tell you I'm about to do? What is my inevitable choice?"

Catrina considered his question. They could head down the road to the right. It was paved and heavily trafficked, full of honking horns and rumbling exhaust pipes. The road to the left was unpaved—a dirt road that ran behind houses. Dots of weeds and wildflowers sprouted among the many puddles. There was no traffic and only one stray dog in sight.

"The road to the left," Catrina replied, knowing Life had never been overly fond of the city bustle and noise.

"Wrong," Life said, and he held out his arm for Catrina. "I choose the road to the right."

"You just did that to prove me wrong!" Catrina laughed as she took her friend's arm.

"No, I actually chose the path before I asked for your opinion."

"Oh?"

"I would have preferred to stroll along the quiet back road."

"I knew it!"

"But," Life went on, "I am well aware of the hard work you put into your gown, and it would surely be damaged if we attempted to navigate all those puddles."

"Nothing I can't mend," Catrina replied. "But thank you all the same."

The friends walked along the paved road, moving aside when traffic overtook them.

"Wouldn't you say I exercised my free will just then?" Life asked. "I acted contrary to what my past suggested I would do."

"True, but there is a reason you made this choice," she said.

"Because I care about you."

Catrina returned Life's smile. "And I appreciate it. Especially because it proves my point."

"How is that?" Life's silver walking stick clicked softly on the road.

"It's simple. When we care for someone, we have *no choice* but to follow our heart, regardless of whether or not we want to."

Life chuckled. "So, given that I care for you, I am forced to make a choice in *your* best interest."

"Exactly! There is no free will where love is involved," Catrina said. "It's like night and day. You cannot have both at the same time."

"An interesting choice of words," Life said. "Considering you have a pendant in your purse that proves the opposite."

"Well . . . that's different."

"Is it, though?"

"It is," Catrina replied. "There is no escaping the commands of the heart!"

The friends waited for the stoplight to give them

the right-of-way. The chaos of morning traffic bustled around them.

"But consider this," Life said. "I may be forced to make certain decisions, given that I care for you. However, I am not forced to care for you. *That* is a choice."

"Hmm." Catrina was considering her response when a wave of music drifted toward them.

"Oh—there!" Catrina indicated a narrow street ahead.

A group of revelers in colorful dresses carried wicker baskets on their heads. The baskets were laden with flowers woven into the shape of stars and moons, crosses and harps. Draped around the revelers' arms and shoulders were beautifully embroidered scarves.

Behind them were musicians playing trumpets and banging on drums. After them came men in white linen shirts and pants carrying enormous papier-mâché figures dancing like giants at a party. And indeed, this was a party.

Calendas were street festivities organized to celebrate any and all occasions, from weddings to the birth of a child to a graduation or a religious holiday. The dancers and musicians moved down the streets, spreading their cheer across the city.

Life and Death joined the parade. The music and laughter were infectious. A young dancer took Catrina's hand and pulled her into the crowd. As she twirled, her skirts fanned out around her, releasing a shower of blossoms. The crowd cheered, and the children ran about collecting the flowers.

The parade took many turns, up and down the winding cobblestone streets. The sounds of the drums bounced against the walls, beckoning people out from their homes, stores, or restaurants to join in the merrymaking.

Life and Death lost themselves to the music and dance, until one of those turns took them past La Casa de Juana. A lone customer peered through the shuttered window. Usually busy at this hour, the restaurant was empty while the family searched frantically for the two missing children. The customer sighed and turned away.

Life sighed as well.

"Alas," he said, "I suppose it's time to resume our game."

Catrina thanked her dancing companion, releasing one more shower of marigolds. The party moved on without them.

"So *that* is what it feels like to be alive!" she said, breathless and almost glowing.

Life smiled.

"What a gift!" Catrina added.

The two friends made their way to the small park across from the robin's-egg-blue house. They set up their table in the shade of a tree and placed their black beans in position. Catrina removed the small mirror from her bag and set it between them on the table.

"I'm ready," she told Life.

Life spoke the riddle for the top card. "ATARÁN-TAMELA A PALOS, NO ME LA DEJES LLEGAR."

"BEAT IT SILLY WITH A STICK, DO NOT LET IT NEAR ME. That's easy," Catrina said. "The spider." She placed a bean on the image of the spider.

Life did the same.

"It appears we are now tied," Catrina told him. "Three in a row!"

CHAPTER 28

"LA ARAÑA"

In the suffocating darkness of her prison cell, Clara crumpled to the ground.

A heavy sob bloomed inside her, tumbling out in a flood of tears.

"I should have gotten help. . . ."

Even as she uttered the words, she knew they were a lie. Had she gone to fetch help when she first saw Esteban disappear, the passage would have closed before she returned.

"And I should have tried harder!"

This, too, was a lie. She had done everything she could to find and rescue Esteban.

"And now we'll never get home."

Before Clara could indulge another thought, some-

thing scraped against the stone in the darkness behind her.

A chill ran down her neck, and her next breath froze
in her lungs. Trembling, she turned around to face the
gaping hole of the cave.

A wave of heat washed over her as a body moved in
the darkness. She took a few steps back, and then some
more, until she could feel the cold metal bars pressing
up against her shoulder blades.

"Help!" she called out to the guards. "There's something in here!"

She pounded on the bars. "Do you hear me!"

Her voice grew louder and more high-pitched, matching her growing panic. *"Help!"*

The silence in the catacombs was dreadful, but not nearly as terrifying as the vision forming before her. Out of the darkness a figure emerged—a shadow within the shadows.

The creature was visible only in spectral contours, but Clara could tell it was enormous by the way it pushed the mass of air toward her. Heat radiated from its body in waves that reminded her of a heart beating furiously.

"Help!" she cried again, frantically pulling on the bars. This time she heard a response, but there were no guards coming to her aid. Instead, there were grunts and groans and growls from other creatures entombed in the many caves surrounding her. It seemed there were hundreds—thousands!—of cells just like hers. And whatever was in them responded to her plea with growls and hisses and claws scraping on stone. She sensed their desperate hunger.

And then Clara realized her mistake. She wasn't a prisoner.

She was lunch.

Clara gasped as the dim light from the corridor revealed the contours of the shadowy creature emerging from the depth of her cell.

What she saw first were two long hairy limbs reaching toward her. These were followed by more limbs and the unmistakable pincers of a massive spider.

Panic flooded her body, lodging in her throat and preventing her from breathing. Her lungs burned as the beast approached.

She pressed herself against the bars, pushing back as far as she could. But it did nothing to distance her from the approaching monster. Behind her the catacombs echoed in hisses and roars, the rumbling of restless creatures.

One of the spider's hairy legs touched Clara, and her body could no longer hold her up. She fell to her knees.

"Please," Clara whimpered. "Please . . ."

There wasn't anything in particular she requested; she simply uttered the only word within her otherwise blank mind.

Clara kept her eyes shut tight, the air around her growing hotter as the spider approached. It made a rapid clicking sound.

It's getting ready to eat me!

A cramp gripped her stomach; her heart raced wildly. The stone floor seemed to be rolling beneath her. The clicking continued, and the spider crept closer.

Clara took a breath, then another. When she took

a third breath, something happened. A small thought sparked within her, so small that she almost missed it.

Esteban.

The thought lit the way for another, brighter thought.

He needs me.

Leading finally to the one that burned like a fiery torch.

I can do this.

And she remembered the rules that governed this place.

A message traveled to her brain, and as the spider's second, third, and fourth legs found Clara, she found the words to change her fate.

"W-wait!" With her head tucked between her knees, she delivered her proposal. "I'll give you something—in exchange for my life. Anything."

The spider towered above her. The shadow of its enormous body forced Clara into an even tighter ball.

"I eat 'em," Clara heard from within her crouched position. Goose bumps prickled across her skin.

"Eat who?" she whimpered.

The spider clicked nosily, then said, "Eedom."

Clara swallowed, forcing herself to push past the lump blocking her throat to make way for the words she needed to say. "I don't understand you." Her voice was muffled by her posture.

Eight feet shuffled around her, scraping against the stone. Heat scorched Clara's back.

"Eedom, eedom!" the spider said. It clicked frenetically.

"Okay, okay," Clara replied. "Calm down. Just . . . give me a moment."

She gathered her thoughts. With her head still tucked between her knees and covered by her arms, her ears were blocked. She was unable to hear clearly.

"P-p-please." Her voice trembled, but she slowly lifted her head. Clara forced herself to open her eyes and said, "Please say it one more time."

"My freedom!" the spider screeched.

Relief gave way to a deep breath filling Clara's lungs, and she eagerly accepted it.

"Your freedom," Clara repeated. "I get it."

With every inhale, her heart became less erratic, and the tension gripping her muscles relented.

"Okay. I need to think," Clara said. "Can you please back away? Just a bit . . ."

She waited until the shuffling feet moved away and a cool breeze swept over her. Then she slowly untangled her body and took a good look at the creature.

The spider was even bigger than she had imagined. Its head nearly touched the cavern's ceiling; its fangs were gnarly and curved inward. In the dim light, Clara could make out most of the spider's body, as big as a small bus, jet-black and streaked with red.

"Thank you." The words were barely a whisper.

The spider responded with a rapid succession of clicks that did not seem entirely friendly.

"First, I need to look around," she said. "So I can figure out what to do."

"There's nothing here," the spider replied. "This is just a giant hole carved into a stone mountain."

Clara eased herself up. "Well, how did you get in here?" she asked.

"I was taken prisoner, like you."

"*You* are a prisoner?"

The spider clicked. "All the creatures here are prisoners." A hairy leg pointed at the catacombs beyond the metal bars. "Slaves, actually."

"Why slaves?"

"El Diablo forces us to work for him." The spider clicked angrily. "He's building an army."

Clara looked back at the rows upon rows of metal bars lining the catacomb walls.

"An army for what?" she asked.

"Enough questions," the spider growled. "I spared your life. I want my freedom."

Clara nodded and took a steadying breath. "I'm not from here," she said. "This information might help me figure out how to escape."

The spider was quiet then, and Clara didn't dare move an inch. Her mind was a jumble of thoughts as she tried to envision a way out.

"What do you want to know?" the spider finally said.

"Why is El Diablo building an army?"

"Las Pozas belongs to a king," the spider explained. "He is said to be a cruel and wicked man. El Diablo is forced to work for him."

Clara's eyes narrowed. "Doing what?"

"Collecting children."

Esteban!

"He delivers them to the king every month at the Mercado Rojo," the spider went on.

"But why? What does the king do with the children?"

The spider clicked angrily. "I have heard he traps them in an underground cavern. That way he can steal their youth—take years of their life for himself."

"*What?*" Clara's yelp rang heavily in the dark space.

Questions swirled in her mind, tumbling one after the other.

"But where does El Diablo find the children?" Clara asked. "How?"

"El Diablo has a key that opens a passageway into the world beyond Asrean. He enters and always returns with a child." The spider shuffled in the darkness. "Sometimes he also brings back creatures for his army: spiders like me, flying scorpions, two-headed dragons."

"Two-headed dragons!" Dread spread through Clara's veins, chilling her to the bone.

"This one had feathers and scales. It blew fire and ice," the spider replied. "And with it came a child."

"What child?" Clara asked.

"A young boy looking for his mother."

"Esteban!" A sob tore through Clara. "El Diablo kidnapped him!"

"No, the children follow him. They go willingly," the spider replied. "It is not hard to trick the broken-hearted."

Clara struggled to breathe.

"Is that all?" The spider clicked impatiently.

"You said there was an army?" Clara replied.

"Yes. El Diablo would like to stop working for the king. He wants to be free."

"That's good, right?"

"It is *not*," the spider growled. "He's been collecting us for years, constraining us to these catacombs with little food or water. Some of us are forced to dig tunnels; others are used for our venom. All are trained to kill upon command. None of us were killers when we came here."

"Oh," Clara whispered. "That sounds awful."

"He's also assembled a troop of human soldiers, mercenaries hired to help lead the attack."

"When?" Clara asked. "Is the attack going to happen soon?"

A surge of hope shot through her veins. But the spider had reached the end of its patience. "I am done answering questions. This is all you need to know. Now *you* must deliver on your end of the bargain."

"I will," Clara said. "Just tell me, please—is the attack going to happen today?"

"It is not," the spider replied. Then it moved closer to Clara. "It will take place during the king's jubilee."

"And when is th—"

"Enough! My freedom for your life," it growled.

"Right," Clara said. "But . . . I don't know how to get out of here."

The spider growled once more. "Well, then, it seems we don't have a deal."

A bloodthirsty chorus arose throughout the catacombs, as if the other creatures sensed an impending attack.

"Stop!" Clara yelled over the din of hungry beasts.

Their calls only grew louder.

"I'm getting hungry," the spider added, and advanced on Clara. "And I don't think you're going to be much use to me alive."

Clara pushed up against the metal bars, with nowhere to go. The darkness of the cave almost seemed to glow behind the massive body moving toward her.

And then she remembered: spiders can't see in the dark.

The conversation with Esteban seemed a lifetime ago, but it gave her an idea.

In one swift motion, Clara pushed herself away from the bars and raced beneath the spider. She zigzagged from one side of the cave to the other, hoping to confuse it. Unfortunately, her white hair was a beacon, reflecting whatever dim light managed to fall through the hole in the cavern ceiling. The spider crawled behind her.

Clara plunged deeper into the cold darkness, diving from shadow to shadow until there wasn't a shred of light to give her away. Her foot hit a soft bulge along one wall, and she quickly moved away from it.

The spider's legs scraped the floor directly behind her.

They can sense vibrations.

Her fingers found a ridge along the wall that opened into a small nook at knee level. It was not large enough to hide her entirely, but it would have to do. She tucked herself into a ball, pressing every inch of skin into the small pocket carved into the stone. She forced her heart to slow down, her breath to quiet, her body to be . . .

Still.

The spider's clicks bounced off the walls as its legs explored the cavern. Clara held her breath as the spider passed by her. A second later, it halted.

"I will find you," the spider said. "There is nowhere for you to go."

Clara tightened every muscle in her body, making herself as compact as possible; she sucked her breath in. But as she pressed herself against the wall, the gravel shifted. A small chunk of stone crumbled and rolled to the ground. Clara squeezed her eyes shut.

A long, hairy leg pinned her against the stone.

"There you are," the spider said. "I told you you wouldn't get far."

CHAPTER 29

IN WHICH ESTEBAN PREPARES TO MEET THE KING

A t three o'clock the door to Esteban's room opened and a man entered, bearing a tray laden with food. His expression was serious, his manner severe. Silently he placed the tray onto the desk and left.

A deepening sense of worry was building within Esteban. He eyed the food suspiciously, but almost as if on cue, his hunger, long dormant, awakened with a roar. The swirls of scents overshadowed any pangs of foreboding. Pan amarillo and requesón; a plate of pineapple, papaya, and melon; chicken in a creamy mole sauce, with rice, black beans, and tortillas on the side; a tall glass of fresh lemonade. A cluster of polvorones sat on a yellow napkin. Esteban eagerly dug in and devoured everything on the tray, down to the last cookie crumb.

Ease washed over him. Thus satiated and comforted, Esteban curled up on the plush bed and took a nap. He slept deeply until he was awakened by the sound of someone moving around in his room.

This time a woman had entered. She, too, wore a serious expression as she tidied up the food and toys. She picked up the remote-controlled car and placed it in the toy box.

"That one is mine," Esteban said. "The man in red gave it to me."

The woman looked up, her eyes gray and heavy. She plucked the toy out of the box and set it back on the desk.

"It's time for your bath," she told him. Her voice was soft and musical, a sharp contrast to her demeanor.

Esteban climbed out of the bed and followed her to the bathroom. Steam had fogged up the mirrors; curls of it danced in beams of golden light. In one corner of the room, steps led up to a large bath piled high with bubbles. Plush white towels lay heaped on the ledge, crowned by a creamy bar of soap.

"In you go." The woman turned around so Esteban

could change out of his clothes. He carefully stepped into the bath, sinking low into bubbles that smelled like vanilla.

"Please wash thoroughly," she said.

Esteban nodded.

"I'll be in the next room setting out your clothes." She scooped up the clothes he had left on the floor and flung them into the garbage. Before Esteban could say a word in protest, she had already left the bathroom.

"My mom made that shirt," he whispered. New clothes were a luxury his family could seldom afford. Fortunately, his mother was an excellent seamstress and able to make gowns out of scraps, suits out of rags, and a new shirt for Esteban out of one of his father's old ones.

Perhaps now that his mother was helping the king, they could have new clothes whenever they needed them.

"Are you soaping up?" the woman called from the next room. "We don't have much time."

Esteban reached for the bar of soap on the towels.

He wanted to give in to the warm water, let its silky smoothness envelop him. But a sliver of doubt gnawed at the back of his mind. He pushed it away.

His mother was probably helping the king with an

important task, which explained why she hadn't yet come to him. The polvorones must have been a gift from her to make him feel better. And she would be so excited to see him, so grateful to the man in red for bringing him to her.

The thought filled Esteban with joy and anticipation. He was eager to see his mother. He was also curious, and more than a little bit excited, to meet the king. He'd never met a king before. He wondered what it would be like to live in a giant palace with everything he could ever want.

With that happy notion, Esteban scrubbed thoroughly, making sure to wash behind his ears and even between his toes. He definitely wanted the king to like him.

Wrapped in one of the plush towels, Esteban walked into the bedroom.

The woman pointed at a crisp white shirt and dark blue trousers. Socks and underwear were set out as well, and on the floor was a shiny pair of black shoes.

"Those are for you," she said.

A jolt of excitement coursed through Esteban. He'd only ever seen clothes as fancy as these on the mayor, when Esteban and his family went to the Zócalo to see the Independence Day celebration. And actually, it was quite possible these clothes were even fancier than those.

"I will return for you in ten minutes," the woman said. "And then we'll go meet your fate."

It was an odd choice of words, and if Esteban had been paying attention, he might have been alarmed. As it was, he was too busy envisioning his mother's embrace to notice anything amiss.

CHAPTER 30

IN WHICH AN ESCAPE IS ATTEMPTED

Pinned beneath the spider, with panic quickly closing in, all of Clara's mistakes bubbled to the surface of her mind.

I should have stayed away from that rose.

I should have controlled my fears in the tunnel.

I should have begged the hunters for a knife.

I should have drawn a horn for the bird.

She stopped.

The horn!

The bird had asked her to draw a horn, and it had said the horn would become real if it liked the drawing. Maybe—

The spider's jaws moved toward Clara.

"Wait!" she gasped, holding up her hands. "I have an idea!"

"I'm afraid the time for ideas is past." The spider clicked. "Now I'm just hungry."

At the mention of hunger, the creatures in the other caves became more frenzied.

"Hold on!" Clara cried. "This might work. And it might be your only chance of getting out of here."

The spider halted. "Is this a trick?"

"No," Clara said. "Please let me explain."

"Okay—talk," the spider said, but it did not retreat.

"Can you at least move your leg?" Clara asked.

"No," the spider replied, and the pressure on Clara's chest increased.

"Fine," Clara gasped. "But don't crush me, or you'll never hear what I have to say."

"Explain!" the spider hissed. "I'm growing weary of you."

Clara explained about the bird and the horn. "Maybe I can draw a key to get us out of here!"

The spider was quiet for a long time, and just as Clara was about to ask if it had heard her, it lifted its foot off her chest.

A rush of cold air flooded her lungs.

"You can try this," the spider said. "But if you attempt to escape again, I will not give you a chance to utter a single word or even take another breath."

"I understand." Clara sat up and leaned her back against the wall. She took a few deep breaths. Her chest ached where the spider had pinned her down, but otherwise she was fine.

"So," the spider urged, "how does this work?"

"I—I'm not entirely sure." Clara quickly added, "But I'm going to figure it out!" She slowly rose to her feet. "First, I need to move closer to the light."

"Remember my warning," the spider said.

Clara rubbed at the sore spot on her chest as she walked toward the front of the cave. Her eyes ran over the ground, scanning it for something she could use as a drawing utensil. But it was all stone, rough and uneven. Even if she did find a stick or a rock, it would be impossible to leave a mark on the floor.

"So?" the spider asked when Clara reached the metal bars.

"I need something I can use as ink," Clara said.

"What about water?" the spider asked. There were plenty of dips and grooves in the stone where water had gathered into pools.

Clara placed her finger into one of the pools. A layer of slime clung to her skin when she pulled her finger back out. She resisted the urge to wipe it away and instead attempted to draw a slimy key on the stone, like the one she'd seen the guard use.

The slime left no mark.

"It's not working," Clara said. "We need something else."

"What about blood?" the spider asked, hovering over Clara.

A chill ran down her spine. "Um . . . maybe."

A sharp pain shot through Clara's arm, and she turned to find an open wound on her skin. "What did you—" She felt dizzy, and the ground seemed to be swaying.

"You'll be fine. I didn't inject any venom," the spider said, then added, "This time."

Clara took a shaky breath and ventured another look at the wound. It was a clean and perfectly round perforation. Inky red blood bubbled to the surface and then began its slow descent down her arm.

"Go on," the spider said. "You're wasting time."

Clara dipped her fingertip into the line of blood.

As she drew the key, the blood, sticky and viscous, stuck to the rock, creating a clearly visible outline.

"Now what?" The spider clicked.

"I don't know," Clara said. "I didn't get this far with the bird."

The spider hissed, and the air around Clara shifted. She turned to see the spider's leg in the air, poised above her head. She twisted her body away just as the spider's leg came crashing down inches from where she stood.

Clink.

Something metallic landed at her feet.

"What was that?" Clara's eyes flew to the spot where she'd drawn the key, the spot where the spider's leg had landed.

"Look!"

Her drawing had materialized in the form of a metal key—a red cylinder with a triangle at one end.

"It must have become real when you touched it," she cried.

The spider clicked furiously but made no move to attack her again.

"Get on with it!" it howled.

Clara grabbed the key and raced to the door. She tried inserting it into the keyhole, but the cylinder was too wide.

"It's too big!" She tossed the key behind the spider into the cave, where it landed with a series of clinks, followed by an agitated rustling.

Clara's heart skipped a beat.

"There's something else back there." Her eyes strained to see into the darkness.

"It's nothing," the spider replied.

But a thought began to take shape. "Oh no." Clara's voice trembled. "Is there another one of you?"

"Let's just say you might want to figure out this key thing sooner rather than later," the spider replied.

Fear bubbled through Clara's veins, and blood dripped down her arm. She touched her fingertip to the red stain, then dropped to the ground and quickly drew another key.

The rustling in the back of the cave grew louder.

"Touch it!" Clara yelled when she finished her drawing.

"It doesn't even look like a key," the spider said. "It's just a mess of lines."

"I didn't say I was an expert," Clara replied.

"Well, then, I don't see how this is going to work." The spider moved closer.

"Just touch it—please!" Her voice echoed loudly, and it was met by a frenzy of clicks from the back of the cave.

"How many of you are there?" Clara choked on the words, but the spider didn't respond. Her arm pulsed with pain.

Finally, the spider touched the drawing and a new key emerged, but this one was too long.

"No, no, *no* . . . ," Clara cried.

"You should probably hurry," the spider said, its voice calm and composed, like a predator waiting for the inevitable to unfold. "The others are far less patient than I am."

"Others!" She took a deep breath. *I can do this.*

Once again Clara gathered blood on her fingertip. She drew a key, narrower and shorter than the last. Then she drew another, of different length, and then a third, a fourth, a fifth.

"Touch them all!" she yelled at the spider as the sound of scurrying feet grew closer.

"I don't know," the spider replied, drawing out each word. "I really don't think you're very good at this."

Clara gritted her teeth. "Enough. You know you want this as much as I do."

The spider sighed. "Fine."

The keys materialized in a sequence of metallic clangs. The first key was still too long, the second key was too short, but the third key . . . slipped right in.

Clara's hand shook as she turned the key. At first it met with some resistance, but

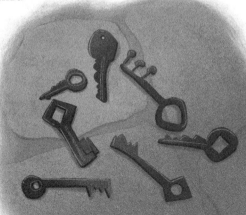

she pushed harder and there was an almost imperceptible click. The metal bars vanished.

Clara gasped. "It worked!"

The spider retreated to the back of the cave, and Clara wasted no time in stepping across the threshold. The catacombs erupted in noise as all the creatures became aware of what had just happened; a deafening roar rocked the stones, momentarily stealing Clara's breath.

Next to the opening of the spider's cave, Clara spotted the round keyhole that would close the metal door. Clutching the key tightly, she moved her hand toward the keyhole.

A promise is a promise.

No matter what.

Despite the fact that the spider had wounded her and given her the scare of her life, it had honored its word. She was bound to do the same.

Clara dropped the key into her pocket and ran as fast as she could.

A moment later, the spider emerged. Crawling along its back were hundreds of newly hatched spiderlings.

CHAPTER 31

IN WHICH THE GAME NEARS ITS END

"What a vibrant place!" Catrina said, scanning the Zócalo, the city's main plaza, which bustled with the activity of many intersecting lives. On one side of the plaza, the cathedral's ornately carved wooden door was open, welcoming people to prayer and reflection. The plaza's other three sides were lined by colorful buildings with elaborate wrought-iron balconies. Bright umbrellas sheltered diners at the restaurants and cafés set around the plaza. The fragrance of café de olla, the traditional ground coffee made in a ceramic pot with cinnamon and raw cane sugar, drifted through the air, momentarily tangling itself with the string of a rouge-red balloon.

"And yet," Catrina sighed, "it is equally cast in such sorrow!"

"The human heart is a delicate thing," Life replied.

They were watching Clara's father, who was speaking with the manager of one of the cafés. Dark circles framed his eyes; his cheeks were sunken, his skin pale. He spoke animatedly as he described his daughter. His eyes begged for news of the girl. The manager shook his head.

"Lo siento," he said.

Life and Death had been following Clara's father as he scoured the city for his daughter. The rest of her family had stayed in Santa María del Tule and formed a search party.

Clara's father had been relentless in his search. The fatigue, hunger, and thirst clearly weighed on him. But it was the possibility of profound loss that made his shoulders sag deeply as he walked to the next café.

"Love is a powerful force," Life said.

"One that is consuming the poor man with grief!" Catrina replied. She turned to her companion. "Surely one cannot *choose* this kind of suffering!"

"What do you mean?"

Catrina explained. "Earlier you said that it was your choice to love me."

"It is." Life smiled.

"But look at what love can lead to." They watched Clara's father exit another café, dejected and clearly heartbroken. "Why would anyone voluntarily agree to such despair!"

"Do not mistake the consequence for the choice," Life replied. "His choice was never to *suffer*—that is the consequence."

"And the choice?" Catrina asked.

"His choice was to *love*."

"More precisely," Catrina said, "his choice was to love *the girl,* for she is who lies at the heart of this drama."

"So you agree?" Life exclaimed. "He had a choice! He exercised his free will when he chose to love his daughter." He grinned and turned to his companion. "Just as I choose to love you."

"You haven't won quite yet." Catrina smiled back. "Let me ask you: Why do you choose to love *me* and not another?"

"Because *you* matter more to me than another. In the same way that his daughter takes precedence in his heart."

Catrina nodded. "And how do you decide what takes precedence?"

Before Life could respond, she went on. "Surely certain things matter to us because of what we have already done and experienced—because of our past. In a way, that makes it inevitable that we should love one over another. Wouldn't you agree?"

"I understand what you are saying," Life replied. "What's more, I see no flaws in your reasoning."

"And yet . . . ," Catrina prompted him.

"I simply cannot accept it as truth." He shook his head to emphasize the point. "To say that I have no choice in whether or not to love you makes love seem . . . insignificant." He paused, gathering his thoughts.

Catrina waited.

"I would say," Life went on, "that the value of my affection for you comes precisely from the fact that it is offered freely. It is a *gift*, not an obligation."

"Perhaps it *is* a gift," Catrina replied. "But it is nonetheless inevitable, given our shared past."

Life sighed. "I will yet figure this out."

"Well, you'd best figure it out soon," Catrina said. "I suspect the end of this game is near."

The friends made their way to one of the many shady trees that lined the plaza. They sat on a bench beneath the tree's heavy boughs and set up their game.

Life gathered the few remaining cards and flipped over the top one. "AL PASAR POR EL PANTEÓN, ME ENCONTRÉ UN CALAVERÓN."

"AS I PASSED BY THE CEMETERY, I FOUND MYSELF A SKULL."

"I like that one," Catrina said.

"Though it seems that neither one of us has the skull," Life replied. He turned over the next card. "UNO, DOS Y TRES, EL SOLDADO P'AL CUARTEL."

"ONE, TWO, AND THREE, THE SOLDIER HEADS TO THE FORT."

This time Catrina placed a bean on the pictograph of a soldier.

CHAPTER 32

IN WHICH ESTEBAN VISITS
EL MERCADO ROJO

E steban followed the man in red out of the castle, through the garden, and down a path that ran directly *into* a waterfall. The water rained down in torrents but parted like curtains when they approached.

A tunnel appeared, lit by an undulating blue coming from some unseen source. The roar of water behind them merged with the roar of water in front, where another fall parted at their approach.

The man in red stepped out and, with a flourish of his arm, pointed at a towering rectangular structure.

"El Mercado Rojo!" he said.

As its name suggested, the building was entirely red, a deep, dark color that clashed violently with the surrounding vegetation. The market was open to the air, with only a roof that was held up by stone towers on all four corners. Vines draped down, creating a screen of green that made it impossible to see inside. The chatter of hundreds of voices mixed with the clink and clang of objects being moved, feet shuffling, and dresses swishing. The market seemed like a beast alive.

"Come," the man in red called out, and Esteban followed him down the path to the market. By the entrance three women sat among large wicker baskets laden with exotic fruits and what looked like insects. One held up a bowl of butterflies.

"Just one, thank you," the man said. He plucked a butterfly from the bowl and popped it into his mouth, biting down with a crunch.

"Ugh!" Esteban groaned.

The woman laughed and turned to greet another customer. For a minute afterward, the man in red floated a few inches off the ground, gliding smoothly among the many stalls.

Inside the market, what had initially appeared to be towers in each corner were now seen to be enormous trees, with branches reaching up and spreading in all directions, connecting in a solid platform that formed the roof.

Everywhere Esteban looked, people were laughing or greeting each other, haggling over wares with vendors at hundreds of market stands.

The stands were simple enough: tables upon which a colorful cloth was draped. The wares, however, were anything but simple.

One vendor displayed bubbles of various colors and sizes, which hovered in place above the table. The colors came from smoke swirling inside the bubbles, making them seem alive. The owner used a long pair of tongs to hold one up for an inquiring customer.

"They're wish-come-trues," the man in red explained. "Each one is unique. See the different colors? The blue ones, azulejos, are small wishes, for easy things that are quick to do, like getting a favorite toy. The green ones, verdantes, deal in feelings, yours or someone else's. The red wishes, fieras, are more volatile; they have some intensity to them and sometimes involve many people."

"What about the black ones?" Esteban asked.

"Those are called negritos. They're special wishes that help you relive a moment in your past."

"And the purple ones?" Esteban pointed at a deep purple sphere hovering between the merchant and his customer as they haggled over the price.

"Mordas are heavy with evil and misdeeds," the man in red explained. "They are curses."

"Two," the customer said.

"Four," the merchant replied.

The customer shook his head. "That's too much."

"Not for what you want."

The customer narrowed his eyes at the merchant, but the merchant stared back unflinchingly.

"Fine, three!" the customer conceded.

"Three it is."

The two men shook hands.

The customer reached into his cloak and pulled out three writhing snakes: a bright green one, a crimson-red one, and a deep yellow snake with a pattern of diamonds running along its skin. He handed them to the merchant, who slipped them into a box at his feet.

Using the tongs, the merchant placed the purple sphere into a velvet bag. He tugged the strings around the bag and handed it to the customer.

The customer quickly slipped the velvet bag into his jacket. With a furtive glance at the man in red, he turned and walked away.

"Let's keep moving."

The man in red led Esteban past a stand that sold upside-down waterfalls ("for going back in time"), a stand with miniature white-capped pine trees ("instant snow makers"), a stand crowded with people hovering over tiny cakes perfectly shaped to look like books ("edible stories").

People bargained and traded: a woman gave up her baby's bonnet; a child, his lollipop. An old man leaned over and whispered something into the ear of a vendor. "A life secret," the man in red whispered to Esteban. "Those are very valuable, especially the older you get."

Esteban's head spun from the crush of sounds and smells surrounding him. He reached for a table to steady himself, but the man in red swiftly grabbed Esteban's hand. "What you touch, you buy. These happen to be quite expensive."

He motioned at the table where Esteban had almost placed his hand. Rows of little wooden bowls were filled to the brim with a murky bluish liquid.

"What are they?"

"Bowls of forgetfulness," the man replied. "You drink from them and you can permanently forget whatever you wish to erase from your memory."

He pointed at a handwritten sign next to the bowls. It was written in a language Esteban couldn't understand.

"It states the price," said the man in red. "Time."

"Time?"

"Days of your life, taken from you."

Esteban took a step back.

"That's right." The man in red smiled. "A steep price to pay."

Alarmed by his near miss, Esteban stayed close to the man in red, following him to a large and lavishly decorated tent set up in the middle of the market. The tarp was a deep indigo and was made of a material that seemed to shimmer. A flap covered the entrance, and two guards stood on either side. Each was dressed in full body armor and held a silver staff. They watched over a line of people waiting to enter the tent. The man in red walked up to the sentries and announced himself. "He's expecting us." The man in red looked at his watch. "In one minute."

The guards nodded. "Wait here."

They waited where the guards had motioned. Esteban's stomach bubbled with excitement, his heart fluttered in anticipation.

"Is my—"

But his question was cut short when a sharp pain exploded within him, releasing a wave of heat and nausea that forced him to double over.

The polvorones had done their job, temporarily numbing him to the anxiety steadily growing inside him. But the effect had finally worn off and, with it, the temporary reprieve Esteban had been enjoying, free of all concerns. Now his premonition hit him full on, like a brutal punch in the stomach. It brought the sour taste of bile to his mouth and all his fears to the surface of his skin, blanketing him in prickly goose bumps.

CHAPTER 33

"EL SOLDADO"

El Soldado

Clara raced up the slippery ramp, peering into each of the cells as she passed. The two-headed dragon the spider had mentioned was her creation. She was sure of it!

Tentacles reached for her through the metal bars of cells she passed; bodies slithered in the darkness; claws scraped across stone floors. But none of the chambers seemed big enough to hold her dragon.

And then she saw it.

Its feathers were silver. Its scales shimmered black. Its eyes were an icy blue.

It was exactly as she had sketched in her notebook, identical to the one on El Árbol del Tule. And it was no larger than the palm of her hand.

Clara approached the small cage hanging from the ceiling. Her dragon fluttered wildly from one side to the other, like a trapped dove.

"What could El Diablo possibly want with you?"

In response, the dragon blew a column of fire so bright it temporarily blinded Clara. A chorus of shrieks and cries ushered forth from all the cells. Deep growls mixed with yowls of pain.

"Right!" Her eyes adjusted to the darkness once the flame died down.

There was no way this dragon could save her, but there was no reason *she* couldn't save *it*.

She pulled the key out of her pocket and inserted it into the keyhole on the cage, hoping it would work. Instantly, the bars vanished.

"Okay, you're free," she told the dragon.

It flapped its wings in place.

"Go on," she urged. "Hurry!"

But the dragon didn't flee.

"I'm sorry," she finally told it. "I have to go. You should go, too."

Clara turned and hurried back down the sloping path, around and around, past all the imprisoned beasts, skidding to a halt at the bottom. As she caught her breath, a whisper of wind brushed her neck. The dragon fluttered at her shoulder, its icy blue eyes peering at her expectantly.

"That's fine," she told the dragon. "You can come with me. But you need to stay close. And be quiet."

Hugging the wall, where the shadows were darkest, Clara made her way toward the decaying stone archway to the left. Beyond it she could see the great hall through which the guards had dragged her when they first brought her in. The dragon hovered over her shoulder, keeping pace with her every step.

Voices echoed off the stone, but she couldn't tell where they were coming from. She sucked in her breath and waited.

The sharp click of boots on stone preceded six black-clad soldiers marching in unison. Metal clasps on their shiny boots clinked in synchronicity. They carried identical rifles, with daggers at the tips—bayonets. Their helmets were a deep red that matched the bands wrapped around their upper arms.

The soldiers hadn't spotted Clara yet, but they were headed straight toward her. Desperately she sought a place to hide. There was nothing but the jagged wall at her back and wet stone at her feet. She thought about running, but the movement would surely be spotted. At least the shadows provided some cover.

Contracting her body as much as possible, Clara pressed herself against the wall. That had worked temporarily in the spider's dark cave. But there was enough dim light in the enormous cavern to illuminate Clara's bone-white hair.

"There!" one of the soldiers called, pointing directly at her. The dragon flitted upward and out of sight. Within seconds, Clara was surrounded.

"How did you get here?" the guard demanded. He pressed the tip of his bayonet to her neck, and she felt a pinprick of pain.

Her mind was blank.

"Feed her to the beasts!" one of the soldiers barked.

Before she could utter a word of protest, a soldier grabbed Clara and began dragging her back to the cell block.

"No! Stop!" she cried, but her voice was drowned out by the scuffling of heavy feet. She recognized it instantly. A moment later, the guards realized what it was, and the blood quickly drained from their faces.

The enormous spider and its battalion of babies surged across the floor and walls like an advancing flood, hungrily crawling toward Clara and her captors.

"Is that—" one of the guards gasped.

The creatures grew frantic in their prisons, eager to partake in the feast. Their hunger made a terrifying ruckus.

One of the guards holding Clara turned and fled. A column of baby spiders raced after him. Before the remaining guards could respond, hundreds of legs and little jaws had fallen upon them. The guards screamed and tried to escape. Clara had no time to do anything but drop to the ground and cover her head.

The spiders crawled over and around her, clicking frenetically as they moved onward. But they left her untouched.

When the wave of arachnids had passed her by, there was nothing left of the soldiers but a pile of limp uniforms and empty helmets, one still spinning in place. The cave echoed with the sound of the spiders' continued onslaught as they encountered more guards and soldiers along the way.

Clara rose and was greeted by the small dragon anxiously flitting around her.

"I'm okay." She took a deep breath and added, "But I'm sure more soldiers will be here any minute." She grabbed one of the uniforms off the floor.

The sleeves were too long, and she had to roll them up; the pants were too big, but she used one of the red armbands as a makeshift belt. She stepped into a pair of boots and placed a helmet on her head, tucking her hair out of sight.

Clara followed the spiders' path of destruction. By the time she and the dragon arrived at the main entrance, she had passed dozens of uniforms and helmets strewn around the cavern floor. The sentry who had been standing guard at the entrance was gone, either consumed by the spiders or having fled the scene. Clara stepped over the threshold and back out into the jungle, where the air was crisp and the sun shone brightly.

She lingered for a moment, basking in the golden light. The lush greenery brought to mind her family's picnic, sitting with Esteban on the warm stone outside la Gruta de Oro, counting butterflies. She could hear the distant echoes of her cousins' voices. She could almost taste the hot chocolate. It seemed an eternity had passed since then.

The rustling of leaves nearby yanked her out of her reverie.

"We need to hurry!" she told the fluttering dragon.

Clara ran down the steps leading into the garden. Keeping well clear of the rose that had betrayed her, she followed the vine-covered walls to the gate at the far end.

From there the jungle fanned into a wild and unruly display of life. Leafy plants vied for space with trees draped in heavy vines. Huge orchids clinging to the trees competed in colorful displays with the many birds perched on the branches. And somewhere in all the greenery, there was a song.

No me olvides, amor.
Nunca estoy lejos de ti.
Tu vida ha sido un dulzor,
Un regalo para mi.

Clara's heart stilled.

"Chita?" she called out.

"Chita?" a voice echoed back.

Clara frowned and searched the trees.

"Who's there?" she asked.

"Who's there?" the voice repeated.

"Don't do that!" Clara said.

"Don't do that!" a bright green parrot squawked from its perch high on a branch.

The startled dragon coughed and sent a flurry of snow onto Clara's shoulder.

"*No me olvides, amor,*" the parrot crooned.

Clara gasped as her aunt's song echoed beneath the canopy.

Nunca estoy lejos de ti.

"Where did you hear that?" Clara asked.

Tu vida ha sido—

"Who taught you that?" Clara called up to the bird. "Answer me!"

The bird jumped to another branch. "Answer me!" it replied.

"That song doesn't belong to you!" Clara yelled.

The parrot disagreed and was of the mind that songs belong to anyone who hears them. It had heard this song coming from a cave one sunny Sunday afternoon many moons ago. The cave, nestled between two worlds, had delivered Chita's words directly to the parrot's ears, almost as if the cave itself were serenading the little bird. The parrot quite liked the song and sang it often. Indeed, it was the parrot's voice that Esteban had heard when he followed the man in red into Asrean.

No me olvides, amor.

"Stop it!" The memory of Chita came upon her with great force, pulling with it a wave of profound sadness. The little dragon hurled a spit of fire at the parrot.

"Stop it!" the parrot yelled back.

"Ugh!" Clara cried. "Stupid bird."

The dragon echoed the sentiment, releasing a cloud of smoke that enveloped the parrot.

The parrot turned its back on Clara, wiggling its body and ruffling its feathers in a show of indignation.

Clara sighed. "I'm sorry. I shouldn't have said that. It wasn't very nice."

"It wasn't very nice," the parrot agreed.

Clara bit her tongue and began walking away, trailing the dragon behind her. But the going was rough, with lush vegetation all around tangling up her legs and making the way impassable.

She turned back and walked in the opposite direction, passing the parrot in its tree once more. That path was equally pointless and impassable. She soon found herself in front of the parrot yet again. Everywhere she looked there was jungle and no clear sign of the Mercado Rojo.

She closed her eyes and balled her hands into fists, squeezing as tight as she could. Then she released her frustration and took a deep breath.

"I can do this," she whispered. "I *will* do this!"

"Do this!" the parrot echoed back.

Ignoring him, Clara looked around. "It has to be here somewhere," she muttered.

"It's here somewhere," the parrot said, and Clara looked up at the bird.

"What did you say?"

"It's here somewhere," the parrot repeated.

"Do you—" Clara studied the bird more closely. "Do you know where it is? The Mercado Rojo?"

"I know where it is," the parrot confirmed.

"You do? That's wonderful!" Clara said. "Look, I'll draw something for you in exchange for you telling me the way."

The parrot waddled on its perch. "Why would I want a drawing? Are you a famous artist?"

"No."

"Are you a *good* artist?"

Clara sighed. "I'm . . . not the best. But the point is that the drawings become real."

The parrot puffed its feathers and uttered a few stunted warbles.

"What would I do with a real drawing by a not-so-good artist?" The parrot laughed.

Clara bristled at the mockery, but she refused to let it distract her. "Listen, if you don't want a drawing, that's fine. What do you want?"

"A trabalenguas," the parrot said.

"A tongue twister?"

The parrot let out a rapid-fire cackle, and the little dragon let out another flurry of snowflakes.

"Yes!" the parrot cried. "That's better than a bad drawing."

"I never said it would be a *bad* drawing. But fine." Clara added, "I'll give you a trabalenguas."

She thought back to that last meal in Chita's sunny garden, when Esteban taught her his new tongue twister.

"Here you go," Clara said. "*Tres tristes tigres, tragaban trigo en un trigal.*"

The parrot shook its feathers and jumped from side to side on its branch. "Oooh! Teach it to me."

She repeated the tongue twister and waited for the bird to recite the words: "Three sad tigers gobbled up wheat in a wheat field."

"*Tres tistres triges,*" the parrot began.

Clara shook her head. "No. *Tres . . .*"

"*Tres.*"

"*Tres tristes.*"

"*Tres tristes.*"

"*Tigres.*"

"*Tigres.*"

"*Tres tristes tigres . . .*"

"*Tres tristes tigres!*"

"Yes, you've got it! Now: *Tres tristes tigres, tragaban trigo en un trigal.*"

"*Tres tistres triges . . .*"

With each passing moment Clara's anxiety grew. But finally the parrot echoed the tongue twister back to her without mistakes. "*Tres tristes tigres, tragaban trigo en un trigal!*"

"Good!" Clara said. "Now it's my turn. Hurry! How do I get to the Mercado Rojo?"

"There," the parrot said.

"Where?" Clara asked.

"There!" The parrot lifted one of its wings and pointed to the right.

Clara paused. "You have to keep your end of the bargain. You can't lie to me," she said. "I already went that way, and it leads to a giant waterfall."

"Waterfall!" the parrot chirped and jumped off its branch, catching a gust of wind.

Riding the breeze, the parrot flew toward the waterfall, with Clara and the dragon racing behind.

CHAPTER 34

IN WHICH THINGS DO NOT AT ALL GO AS EXPECTED

Esteban's stomach was a tight knot. He moaned and clutched his belly, trying hard to keep the contents of his last meal from spilling out onto the floor.

"You're nervous," the man in red told him. "It's normal. Meeting a king is a big event."

Esteban nodded, although he didn't think his nausea had anything to do with meeting the king.

"Is my mom in there?" He groaned. "Maybe you can ask her to come out for a moment."

"She's busy right now," the man replied. "Just take deep breaths and try to calm your nerves. Here, have another cookie."

A polvorón materialized in his hand.

"I don't think I—"

Before he could finish his sentence, the man popped the cookie into Esteban's mouth. The sweetness dissolved on his tongue. As it did, the knot in his stomach also dissolved, and he was flooded with a sense of welcome ease and calm.

Esteban took a few deep breaths.

"Better?" the man asked.

Esteban nodded. However, even though the feeling of anguish had vanished, the idea of it remained, and he wondered why he was so worried.

Esteban believed what the man in red told him, that his mother was waiting for him. He'd heard his mother's song in the jungle. She was here, somewhere. Still, it was odd that she hadn't come to find him or even sent a message.

A thought took shape in his mind. Perhaps she didn't know he was here. Maybe she was too busy helping the king, and this would be a surprise for her. Esteban liked that idea, and he held on to it tightly.

But how, he wondered, had the king found out about her? And why had she left without telling anyone, especially since they all thought she had died?

These were problematic questions for which he

didn't really want answers, so Esteban turned his attention to the line of people queuing up behind them.

Some carried baskets or bundles laden with goods. Others were hauling things in carts or in sacks draped on the backs of animals. One old man wore a white tunic and held an ornately decorated ceramic urn from which a long swirl of smoke arose. The smoke changed colors, from shimmering white to blue to pink and back to white. Sparks of glitter crackled within it. A chain of gold tethered the swirl to the old man's hand.

"What is that?" Esteban asked the man in red.

"It's the tail of a Soul Devourer. You pour it into your enemy's mouth, and it will consume their soul. It's quite valuable. People kill, literally, for a gift like that."

"Why are they giving the king gifts?"

A frown flitted across the face of the man in red but was quickly replaced. "Perhaps *gift* is not the right word," he said. "Let's call them payments."

The tent flap opened, and a woman stepped out. One half of her face was young, with soft skin and a bright blue eye. The other half was ancient, wrinkled and spotted with age, with sagging skin around a dull, cloudy eye. She pulled a hood over her head and covered the old half of her face so that only her youthful side could be seen. She nodded at the man in red as she passed.

"You may enter," the guard said. The man in red took hold of Esteban's right arm. At the same moment a soldier grabbed Esteban's left arm.

"Run!" The soldier yanked Esteban hard and pulled him out of the grasp of the man in red.

"Let go!" Esteban cried, trying to wrench the soldier's hand off his arm.

But the soldier gripped him hard and pulled, dragging Esteban away.

"Stop them!" the man in red shouted from behind.

People reached for Esteban, but the soldier quickly evaded them: turning tight corners, ducking behind carts or barrels, knocking people over in their path.

A long wooden pole suddenly jutted out from one of the stalls, hitting the soldier in the stomach. The soldier yelped and doubled over, bringing Esteban to a quick halt and momentarily releasing him.

Esteban began to run away.

"Wait," the soldier gasped. "Esteban!"

At the sound of his name, he stopped. The soldier's helmet had fallen off, and a curtain of white hair covered the person's face. The soldier looked up.

"*Clara?*" Esteban gasped.

Before he had a chance to say anything else, his arm was firmly in the grasp of the man in red.

"Thank you, sir," the man in red spoke to the owner

of the wooden pole, who now had Clara in his custody. "For your troubles." He handed over a gold coin in exchange for Clara.

"I recognize you," he said, through gritted teeth. His free hand closed around her arm, and his nails dug into her skin.

Clara recalled the piercing stare of his eyes through the wall of vines. She shivered as their eyes locked once more.

"Esteban!" Clara cried. "I've come to rescue you."

"Is that so?" said the man in red. And he laughed and laughed, dragging the two children back to the blue tent, where the king awaited.

Unseen by the man in red, the two-headed dragon also waited, nestled deep in Clara's pocket.

CHAPTER 35

IN WHICH THERE IS A WINNER

"Oh, dear," Catrina sighed. "Things do not seem to be progressing well for the children."

"I'm afraid not," Life agreed.

"And we are down to just a few cards." Catrina indicated the now-diminished pile in the center of the table.

Life pointed at the top card. "Perhaps the next card will determine the child's fate."

"Correction." Catrina held up a bony finger. "Her fate was determined long ago. It will simply be revealed."

Life chuckled, but he did not flip over the card just yet.

The two friends were relishing the perfect summer evening unfolding in the Zócalo. Children raced among the trees and bushes playing hide-and-seek, their laughter giving them away as clearly as an X on a map. Lanterns suspended from heavy branches all around the plaza bloomed into life as a man lit them each with a long match. A lone guitarist sat on the lip of a bubbling fountain, offering his love ballad to all who were within hearing range.

"Are you ready?" Life asked.

"Not really." Catrina turned back to her companion. "But I suppose we have no choice."

Life chuckled. "I daresay, my dear, you may have found your winning argument." He shook his head and flipped over the next card. "EL SOMBRERO DE LOS REYES."

"THE HAT OF KINGS," Catrina said.

"The crown." Life placed his bean on his board, completing a row of four and bringing the game to an end.

"The crown, indeed," Catrina said. She set down the black bean beside her tabla. "And so it seems we have a winner." She nodded at Life. "Congratulations, my friend."

CHAPTER 36

"LA CORONA"

La Corona

"**L**et me go!" Clara strained against the tight grip of El Diablo.

"Don't worry, Clara," Esteban said. "He's going to take us to see my mom."

"No, Esteban, you can't trust him! It's a trick!" she cried. "He's taking you to the king."

"I know," Esteban said. "That's where my mom is."

El Diablo moved through the crowd with ease, one hand holding Esteban's and the other dragging Clara by the arm.

"Esteban, you don't understand!" Clara cried. "The king *collects* children!"

"Yes," Esteban replied. "He takes them to his castle,

where there are toys and books and lots of good things to eat. He takes care of the children."

"No!" Clara groaned. "That's not it at all."

But Esteban wasn't listening. "And he invites the children's mothers to go with them. That's where my mom is, you see? She didn't die, like everyone said. She went to the king's castle to get everything ready for me."

"She's not—"

"And I heard her singing! She was calling to me! She guided me here!" His voice rose with every word.

"No!" Clara cried. "Esteban—listen to me. It wasn't her. It was a parrot."

"What?"

"It was a parrot," Clara repeated. "Not Chita. I saw the parrot."

"I don't think that's right." Esteban shook his head, then went on chattering. "Clara, I can't wait to see her. And I know she'll be so happy to see you, too."

She struggled to pull free of El Diablo.

"Help!" Clara yelled. "Someone help! He's kidnapping us!"

The crowd ignored her cries, graciously moving aside for El Diablo. Some even bowed their heads or curtsied.

"This is my home," El Diablo told Clara, his voice

silky smooth. "And everyone here is a guest of mine. They will pay you no mind. Now please stop making this so difficult. It won't change a thing."

Clara knew he was probably right, but she wasn't about to make things easier for his sake. She continued crying out and struggling until they reached the king's tent. El Diablo walked up to the guards and said, "With apologies for the delay, please tell him I bring him *two* offerings today."

One of the guards nodded and slipped in through the tent flap.

"You can't do this," Clara told El Diablo. "We don't belong to you."

The guard returned and held the tent flap open. El Diablo stepped through, dragging Clara and Esteban behind him.

The tent was much larger on the inside than it was on the outside. It looked like a proper throne room, with a black marble floor polished to such a shine that it gave the impression of walking on a mirror. The walls were covered in gold leaf, which reflected the glow of floating pockets of fire lighting the room. The walls rose and met in a domed ceiling far higher than the tent appeared to be on the outside. Gems were encrusted in the ceiling in various geometric patterns. Esteban noticed there were also diamonds buried in the polished surface of the black marble floor. A low hum of conversation issued from elegantly dressed people speaking in hushed voices; servants moved among them, carrying food on silver platters and pouring drinks from crystal water pitchers; a large table against one wall held a feast fit for a king and all his army.

On a dais in the center of the room stood a large golden throne flanked by lush palms. Two enormous guards dressed in full battle array stood on either side of the king, who was no older than Clara. He had piercing green eyes and jet-black hair. His skin was smooth and seemed to glow, reflecting the warm light from the fires lining the walls. He wore a thick blue tunic studded with sapphires, and on his head sat a silver crown with jagged peaks that splintered the light in all directions.

"My king," El Diablo said.

Clara dug her heels in as he dragged her forward, but the marble floor was as smooth as ice and offered no grip.

"You mentioned something about an extra offering today," the king said.

"It is your lucky day." El Diablo shoved Esteban forward. "This child is eight."

"And the girl?" the king asked.

El Diablo tightened his grip on Clara's arm. "She is eleven. Combined, that's a lot of years."

"Good," the king said. "Take them." He gestured to one of the giants at his side.

With a heavy clang of metal, the giant stepped off the dais and grabbed Esteban.

"*Ow!*" Esteban squirmed in the guard's iron grip. "That hurts," he whimpered. "Please stop."

But the guard didn't release Esteban. Instead, he reached for Clara, crushing her arm in his giant hand.

"I thought you loved children," Esteban said to the king.

"I do," the king replied. His lips turned upward, into a grin that could only be described as sinister. "Very much."

"Well . . . I'm off, then," El Diablo said.

The king nodded.

"Wait!" Esteban called out. "What about my mother? When do I get to see her?"

El Diablo walked away without another word.

Esteban turned to the king. His voice was barely a whisper. "When do I get to see my mother?"

The king frowned. "Your mother? I don't know anything about your mother."

Esteban groaned as the pain took shape within him,

first as a knot in his belly and then spreading through his body.

"Esteban?" Clara attempted to reach him, but the guard kept her firmly in place. Esteban began to cry.

A sheen of sweat coated his skin. "I don't feel so well."

And with that, all the anguish that had been dulled by the polvorones exploded within him. He dropped to his hands and knees and proceeded to be sick on the marble floor.

A servant girl raced over to clean up the mess.

Without another glance at the boy on his knees, the king called out, "Bring in the next one!"

Esteban was sobbing now, overwhelmed by the weight of his premonition. Clara struggled in vain to free herself from the guard's grasp as they were led toward a spiked metal door.

"What's happening?" Esteban cried. "Where are they taking us?"

Clara knew what was happening, but she wasn't going to break her cousin's heart again by disclosing what the spider had shared with her.

The spider!

"Wait!" she called out, remembering an important detail the spider had given her.

But the guard continued dragging her toward the metal door.

"Stop!" she yelled. "I have something to say to the king!"

Another guard reached for the door handle.

"Your Highness!" Clara screamed. "I have important information! It could save your life."

The king turned toward them.

"*Halt!*"

Everyone froze, and in the silence that followed, the king spoke.

"What did you say?"

"I have important information," Clara repeated.

"Well, what is it?"

"Someone is plotting against you!" Clara said. "And I have details."

"Bring them back!" the king commanded.

The guard did as he was bidden.

"So." The king's eyes glinted sharply. "What information do you have?"

Clara shook her head. "Nothing is free in this world. You need to give me something in return."

The king narrowed his eyes. "What do you want?"

"Our freedom," Clara said. "You let us go home, and I tell you everything I know."

The king was silent. He stared at Clara without blinking. His sharp green gaze drilled into her, but she kept her eyes steady and refused to look away.

"Very well. I will grant you your freedom."

Clara felt buoyant with relief.

"Well?" The king's eyes flashed.

She took a deep breath and approached the throne. Into his ear she whispered everything the spider had confided about El Diablo's plan to attack.

"Is that so?" he asked.

Clara nodded.

The king said nothing for a long time.

"Treachery!" His voice bounced off the chamber walls with such force that Clara flinched and Esteban let out a cry.

"No more visitors!"

The king barked orders. "Send everyone away. And bring me my generals!"

"What about us?" Clara asked.

The king dismissed her with a wave of his hand. "Take these two to the tunnel. And bring me El Diablo!"

"Wait!" Clara cried as the giant guard pulled her away and back toward the metal door.

"We had a deal!" she yelled, but it was in vain.

The guard heaved open the metal door, revealing a

black river running through a tunnel stained with shadows and decay. A small canoe bobbed in the dark water, tethered to a ladder next to the door. Clara and Esteban were unceremoniously dropped into the boat.

The king's throne room was promptly cut off as the door closed heavily with a thud.

CHAPTER 37

IN WHICH LIFE
AND DEATH MEET CLARA

Life and Death gazed into the silver circle between them, watching the children plunge into darkness. The moment called for silence, and the friends honored it in stillness.

"What a tragic result," Catrina finally said. She swept the mirror into her bag as Life packed up their tablas.

"And you must now redeem your prize," she went on. "A long life for the child."

Life sighed and shrank the deck into a single card, El Catrín.

Catrina gathered the frijoles before adjusting the crown of never-wilting flowers on her head.

They rose from their makeshift table. Life folded the monogrammed red handkerchief neatly into a perfect square and returned it to his jacket pocket. Then he offered Catrina his arm.

Laughter spilled from one window; from another, a baby's cry was hushed. A car rumbled along the street, bumping over potholes. The city was just as alive at night as it was during the day: streetlamps took the place of sunlight, casting diners in a soft orange glow matched by flickering candles on restaurant tables; peals of laughter mingled with love ballads; wings dominated the sky as bats replaced the birds.

"I will miss this town," Catrina sighed.

"As will I," Life agreed.

"And I will miss you."

Life reached over and squeezed Catrina's hand resting on his arm.

"Shall we?" he asked.

She nodded.

Life and Death were not subject to the constraints of time and place. For beings such as them, moving between worlds was a simple matter of snapping one's fingers. Thus, with a snap, the colorful facades and giant jacaranda trees were quickly replaced by the darkness of a dripping tunnel.

"Watch your step," Life said as he led Catrina to a

canoe tethered to a hook in the wall. Clusters of green flames hovered along the tunnel wall, casting an eerie light onto the black river.

The two companions took their places, and the boat began to move, retracing the path it had followed for centuries through the inky water.

Life and Death were silent; the only sound was that of water splashing along the canoe and the crackling of fire. A whimper made its way toward them, but it quickly receded, lost to the watery tunnel.

Catrina plucked an embroidered fish from her dress. It leaped into the river, where it glowed like an underwater lantern, projecting an orange halo of warm light along the tunnel walls. Critters scurried around and overhead, fleeing the passing light.

"It's rather dismal in here," Catrina noted.

"That is an understatement, my dear," Life replied. "But where are the children?"

No sooner had he asked the question than the glow of the fish provided the answer. The tunnel opened out into a massive cavern containing a black lake. A cone of cold, misty light spilled from an opening in the cavern's domed ceiling, revealing hundreds of small floating islands. Made from little more than twisted plants and roots, they were just big enough for one child each.

The children were subdued, their eyes haunted, their bodies still and quiet. Those on the islands closest to the entrance were newly arrived. Their eyes still held the glow of youth; their bodies looked strong and healthy. The children farthest from the entrance wore a lifetime of wrinkles and gray hairs. Their withered bodies were weak and frail.

"This is outrageous." Catrina's voice fled through the opening overhead. "An atrocity!"

A red canoe traveled from island to island. It was empty except for a black urn that contained a long silver needle. One by one, each child held out a fingertip as the canoe approached them. The needle rose from the urn, then hinged to position itself directly over the soft flesh of the child's fingertip. Swiftly it pierced the skin, extracting a drop of blood and sucking it into the urn before moving on to the next child.

The fingertips of the children who had been there longest were callused and scarred. They scarcely felt the prick of the needle. The newer arrivals, on the other hand, had skin that was still soft and tender.

"Ouch!" a child gasped as the needle collected her blood and, with it, a year of her life.

Following behind the red canoe, a green vessel delivered a small ceramic bowl containing a meager meal of beans and rice. As the child gathered her food, a sigh escaped her lips, floating across the water toward the boat with Life and Death. The sigh quickly sank into the dark waters and was silenced.

"There!" Catrina pointed at an island just big enough for Clara to sit cross-legged.

"Don't cry," Clara whispered. She reached out her hand toward Esteban's small island, but the distance between them was too great.

"It's going to be fine," she added.

"No, it's not!" Esteban cried. "There's nobody here to help us."

"I'm here," she said.

Esteban nodded. "But there's nothing you can do." His small voice filled the cave with profound sadness. "We're stuck here."

The red boat with the urn drifted up to them, and the needle rose to prick Esteban's finger. He moved away, trying to evade it, but the needle followed him and quickly found its target. His blood was drawn into the urn. As soon as the deed was done, the green boat delivered a bowl of food to Esteban.

The red boat then approached Clara's island, and the urn collected her blood. The days drained from her body, like air being stolen from her lungs. Her skin

tightened, her fingertips wrinkled. An emptiness grew inside her, vast and heavy with despair.

How had she ended up in this hopeless place? She thought of all the wild twists and turns, the events that had led her, almost by the hand, to this very cavern. How could she have done anything differently? What choice did she have?

The hollowness inside Clara spread, and as it did . . . it revealed something.

To believe—despite everything. To have hope. *That* was a choice.

"Esteban," she said. "You're right to say that we're stuck here."

Esteban whimpered.

"But you're wrong to think there's nothing I can do."

"What do you mean?"

"Look, I made you a promise, remember? I told you I would always take care of you."

Esteban nodded.

"When you vanished from the garden, I didn't break my promise, did I?" She didn't wait for him to answer. "No. I followed you into this bizarre world.

"And I followed you through that wild jungle, past that ridiculous wall of vines, and into the enchanted castle."

He blinked back tears.

"And even though there was nobody there to help me, I managed to escape that awful spider's lair, and I found you at the Mercado Rojo."

"What spider?"

Clara laughed as hope bloomed within her. "Don't you see? There was always something standing in my way—all these unexpected and dangerous things. But they didn't stop me. I still tracked you down. Do you know why?"

"Why?"

"Because I made you a promise."

Esteban sniffled.

"And I'm going to keep it," Clara added.

"But—but what are you going to do?"

Clara squeezed her fingertip where the needle had pricked her. She gathered another drop of blood. Before the pinprick dried on her fingertip, she drew a figure eight on her palm. Then she touched it. A butterfly with ruby-red wings rose from her hand.

"What is it?" Esteban asked.

"It's right here. Can't you see it?"

"It's too dark." Esteban squinted into the darkness.

"Oh . . . ," Clara sighed. "Well, it's . . . It's supposed to be—"

The tiny dragon rose out of Clara's pocket and blew a spot of fire onto the butterfly's wings.

"A butterfly!" Esteban cried.

It was an impossible thing, and yet there it was: hope dancing brightly in the darkness.

Quickly, Clara drew another, and another. The dragon breathed on their wings, making each of the butterflies glow. Children on the neighboring islands began to notice the growing kaleidoscope of light; their faces gazed at the swarm in wonder, and a quiet murmur of laughter rippled among them.

"They're beautiful," Esteban said, his face reflecting the glow of dozens of blinking wings.

"We may be stuck," Clara said once more, "but for as long as we're here, this place will be filled with so much magic you won't even care." She squeezed another drop of blood and with it drew a cluster of roses.

The dragon sprinkled them with snow, and the crystalized flowers beamed with silver light.

"We will have birds and fish, unicorns and fairies." She turned to Esteban. "We will have a galaxy of stars!"

And the little dragon blew sparks of fire into the air.

Esteban smiled, and his grin spread to the faces of all the other children.

"You see?" Clara said. "We're going to be fine."

It was then that she spotted Life and Death.

There is a moment in everyone's life, right before we veer in an unexpected direction, when we sense that everything is about to change. The moment may be subtle, and we may not even realize what's happening. But our skin tingles, and time slows down. Our next breath heralds a fundamental shift in the world as we know it. And so it was with Clara as she watched Life and Death approach.

Life brought the canoe to a halt before her. He removed his hat and bowed.

Catrina, flush in all her beauty, inclined her head as well. In a barely audible voice, she sighed, "Poor children."

"We've already given our blood," Clara told them.

Life shook his head. "We are not here to take your life."

"What do you want, then?"

"To give you this." Catrina held out the pendant. The white side was facing up, and light rose from the small circle, illuminating the cavern with moonlight.

A child on a nearby island gasped.

Catrina flipped the pendant over to the black side.

Sunlight glowed from her palm. It lit up the years of moss and mold and drippings that had flourished on the dark walls, but it also filled the cavern with unexpected warmth.

"It's beautiful." Clara accepted the token. "Thank you."

"We also offer a prize," Life added.

"A prize?" Clara frowned. "Is this a trick?"

Life shook his head. "This is no trick, child. We are here to grant you the gift of a long life."

"A *long* life?" Clara pulled back. She swung her gaze around the dark cave and the islands with haunted children. "Here?"

Life sighed.

"I—I thought you said this was a prize." Clara's voice trembled. "That's not a prize; it's a punishment." She moved as far back as she could on her little spot of floating mud. "I don't want anything from you."

"It is yours, and you must accept it," Life replied.

"Why me? Give the prize to someone else, someone in a different place."

"We didn't choose you, child," Catrina explained. "A cold and ancient breeze, shaped by forces far more powerful than us, found a window opened at just the right time."

"It was pure chance," Life said.

"I would say it was destiny," Catrina replied.

Clara recalled that morning, so very long ago, when she found a tangle of silver wrapped around her braids.

"But . . . I didn't ask for any of this," she said.

"Indeed, destiny cares little for our desires," Catrina replied.

"Well, I don't want your prize," Clara said. "Or your gift." She held out the pendant, but Catrina refused it.

Resigned to a truth he could not deny, Life whispered, "I'm afraid you have no choice."

Clara blinked rapidly. "But why not? I don't understand." The acoustics of the cavern amplified her words.

"Life dealt you these cards," Catrina said. "It is how your story unfolds." She paused briefly before adding, "You've never had a choice."

Clara thought back to all that had transpired in the last days. It was true, in a way. She hadn't had a choice about the tree or the scorpion or Chita dying; or about Esteban being transported to this world; or about her being trapped by the vines and captured by El Diablo's men. And there were other things, events that had happened long before that fateful day when she opened the window and heard the bells toll.

It all led her to this place, and she hadn't had a choice about any of it.

"W-well . . ." Her voice trembled, matching the

tremors running through her body. "What about you?" She turned to Life. "Do you have a choice?"

Life startled.

"Do you *have* to give me the prize?" Clara asked.

In all the years upon years, centuries upon centuries, nobody had ever asked him this question. He had never considered that *his* choices were as pre-determined as those of the human pawns at the center of their game.

"I—"

"It's unavoidable," Catrina said. "This game must end." She turned to Life. "Or there cannot be another."

Catrina looked at Clara and shook her head. "I'm sorry. We *must* give you the prize. It's the only way."

"Then give me something else," Clara begged. "Anything other than a long life in this—this awful place." Her voice cracked. "Surely *that's* a choice you can make."

Life turned to Catrina. A smile played on his companion's face.

"How clever," Catrina said.

"What would you have me give you, then?" Life asked.

Clara didn't hesitate. "A wish," she said. "I wish that none of this had ever happened."

Life shook his head. "You cannot change the past. It is what it is. I could send you back to the day this all began, but things would unfold in exactly the same way, and we would find ourselves here once more, facing the very same dilemma."

"There is no point in reliving such sorrow," Catrina added.

"Well, then . . ." Clara looked around at all the children. "I wish for you to free us. Send all of us home, back where we came from."

Life sighed, a deeply regretful sound. "Those are multiple wishes, one for each. I can gift only one."

"So . . . you can free only one of us." Clara's voice was hardly a whisper.

"If that's what you want," Life said.

"It is," Clara replied. The words carried a certainty she had not felt in a very long time, and she spoke them before her fear caught up with her. "I wish for you to save Esteban. Send him to my parents, make him forget everything that happened."

"Clara!" Esteban cried. "No. I won't leave without you."

Clara turned to her little cousin, her number one fan and supporter; the one who had always known, even when she herself did not, that she was the brave one, capable of great things. She looked at all the giggling children reaching for the butterflies.

"Listen," she told Esteban. "And remember this: we may not have a choice about what happens to us.

We didn't ask for any of this." She extended her arm, pointing across the lake. "We didn't choose to end up in this dark and broken place. But there is nothing we can do to change the fact that this is where we are."

Esteban sobbed quietly.

"The thing is, even if we had no choice about what happened to us, we still get to decide what to do about it." Clara pointed at the butterflies blinking overhead. "I *choose* not to let the terribleness of this place be the end of my story. Or yours."

She turned back to Life. "I've made my decision. I want to free Esteban."

Life nodded. There was no flash of lightning or

shimmering in the air, no tear in the fabric of time. Life simply held out his hand to Esteban and helped him into the small boat.

"I love you!" Esteban cried.

"I love you, too." Clara forced the words past the tight knot in her chest.

She pushed the canoe away. Life gave her a small nod, and a petal drifted off Catrina's crown of roses as she inclined her head in parting. The petal floated on the dark water for a brief moment before being devoured by the lake.

Clara watched the boat until the tunnel swallowed up the three figures. And then her heart split open, flooding her in sorrow.

CHAPTER 38

IN WHICH THERE IS AN UNEXPECTED TWIST AND A CONUNDRUM

As the canoe traversed the dark tunnel, it fell into a gently swaying motion that lulled Esteban to sleep. It was in this state of slumber that Life plucked out Esteban's memories, one by one, and dropped them into the river, where they quietly dissolved. But he made sure to keep Clara's parting words intact. *Even if we had no choice about what happened to us, we still get to decide what to do about it.*

Despite all odds, despite the unbroken chain of events that had led the girl to this one moment over which she had no control, she had nevertheless managed to make a choice.

As if she were reading his thoughts, Catrina said, "Remarkable."

Life looked up at her.

"I did not expect to find such hope and courage amidst so much darkness," Catrina said, turning her gaze back down the tunnel toward the cluster of islands.

Life nodded. Even at this distance they could pick up the red glints of butterflies.

"Or the ultimate proof of free will," Catrina added.

"The girl's choice?" Life asked.

Catrina shook her head. "No. Yours."

"Mine?"

A smile spread across Catrina's face.

"All this time," she said, "thousands of years, we've been trapped in this endless game, trapped in this endless conversation."

Life nodded, urging her on.

"We always seek a pawn over whom we deliver an inevitable verdict. Never once did we consider that we— not the people with whose lives we play—are the pawns in this game." She shook her head and laughed.

And it was true. The game always followed the same rules: a victim was identified, never chosen; the cards were shuffled and flipped, never chosen; the result was inevitable, never chosen.

"And yet today," she went on, "for the first time in

eternity, a choice has been made. *You* chose a different fate for the child."

Catrina paused, and a deep silence marked the enormity of what had transpired.

"I suppose you're right," Life finally conceded. "Although it is not a fate to be envied."

"No, indeed, it is not," Catrina replied. "But I wonder. There may yet be a way out for the girl."

"A way out?" Life asked.

"Another choice to be made," Catrina said.

In his slumber, Esteban stirred, mumbling something unintelligible. "My dear friend," Catrina said. "The girl may think her ultimate choice was granting the boy's freedom. But she made another, even more important choice."

"Oh?"

Catrina pointed across the water. "You and I, we look around and see darkness and despair. The girl, she looks at the same thing but sees hope. We see the inevitable conclusion of a game; she sees an opportunity to transform."

Catrina turned back to Life. "She is bound by the same circumstances that enslave all the children here, but she chooses to see a different paradigm, one in which she need not be defeated."

Defeated. The word echoed down the tunnel, away from the canoe slipping through the darkness.

"What's more," Catrina went on, "her choice liberated you."

"In what sense?"

Death smiled. "We have been playing this game for an eternity, constrained by what we thought to be its strict rules."

"The rules are unchangeable," Life said.

"In the same way that the children's present circumstances are unchangeable." She pointed toward the children's islands. "These circumstances may describe the moment, but they do not define it."

"So what defines it?"

"The choices they make."

Life looked past Catrina toward the dots of islands in the distance.

"This place is what it is: a cavern of squalor, despair, and hopelessness," Catrina continued. "But the girl's choice also makes it a place of beauty and wonder. In so doing, she has given these circumstances a different meaning."

"And the game?" Life asked.

"It, too, is what it is," Catrina replied. "But your choice has given it a different meaning; it has opened up a world of opportunities for those who receive your gift."

Life nodded.

"And it opens up a world of opportunities for us as well," Catrina added.

"How so?"

Catrina sat up straighter and fanned her skirts around her. "I, too, choose to give this game a different meaning."

She adjusted the crown of flowers on her head. "But we must go back and speak to the girl. In the end, it is she who must decide."

CHAPTER 39

IN WHICH ONE STORY ENDS, AND A NEW ONE BEGINS

It had been only an hour, though it felt as if an entire lifetime had been lived. The boat drifted to a stop at its mooring. Catrina stepped out first, and Life followed, carrying Esteban in his arms. Once they were on steady ground, Life snapped his fingers, whisking them away from the king's castle and depositing them in Chita's backyard, where the sun was just announcing its morning arrival.

Neighbors and family alike had searched Santa María del Tule and the surrounding towns through the night for Clara and Esteban. Not an hour earlier, the last of the search party had withdrawn to catch a few hours of sleep. They slumbered fitfully, blanketed in sadness.

In the kitchen, Juana had fallen asleep at the table

while making tortillas in preparation for another day of searching. Her head rested on her arm, covered in masa flour, and in her hand she clutched a ball of dough.

The movement of Catrina's dress as it brushed against the plants startled Juana out of her sleep. She sat up and looked out the window, where she saw a beautiful woman and a dapper man holding Esteban in his arms.

"Oh!" she gasped, and raced out to the garden. "You found him!"

Life nodded and handed the sleeping boy into Juana's waiting arms. Her eyes asked a question that her lips could not yet formulate.

"We didn't find the girl," Catrina said, which was a lie, of course, but kinder than the truth.

Catrina had returned to the island and given Clara the choice of death—to join her then and escape her circumstances altogether. But Clara had refused, not because she feared death. Rather, it was "for the children," she had said. "If I go now, they'll be all alone." She pointed at the kaleidoscope of firelit wings flitting from island to island. Small hands reached out playfully, a giggle caught flight on a cold gust of wind. "If I stay, I can at least give them . . . something."

"Hope," Catrina said.

Clara had nodded, and with that she sealed her fate.

"I'm sorry," Life now told Juana.

Juana sighed deeply. "Thank you for bringing him home." Then she added, "Would you like some coffee or . . . something to eat?"

Life shook his head. "You're kind to offer, but it's been a long night and it's time for us to go."

"I understand." Juana nodded.

Life and Death watched as Juana carried Esteban into the house and set him gently on the couch. They watched as she covered the boy with a warm blanket and sat down beside him, placing her hand protectively against his body.

"It seems our work here is done," Life said.

"I believe it is," his partner agreed.

Life, dressed in his black suit and vest with a crisp white shirt and the tiniest hint of red peeking out of his jacket pocket, smiled at his companion.

"Until we meet again."

"Until then." She gathered a blossom from her crown and pinned it to his lapel.

He gave a solemn bow, and with a snap of his fingers, the two friends vanished.

Esteban would wake many hours later with no recollection of what had transpired during his fateful journey to Las Pozas. The only vestiges of the adventure were a deep ache in his heart whenever he thought of

Clara and a vague image of butterflies glittering in the darkness.

The family never stopped searching for Clara, and Clara did return—one last time.

After Life and Death had departed the cavern, taking Esteban with them, Clara continued to share her magic with the children. The two-headed dragon stayed faithfully by her side, breathing light into her creations. In this way the years drained from her body as the cavern filled with stars and dragonflies, fish with wings, and birds with petals for feathers.

But for every flutter of glowing wings or sprig of snowcapped roses, her heart would suffer the knowledge of life fleeing her body. Within two months, she was an old woman. Sometimes despair would fall upon her, threatening to crush what little hope she kept alive. Then she would place the black-and-white pendant on her palm to give them all a moonlit moment or the memory of the rising sun.

As for the king, in an inevitable turn of events (for it is well known that every act has consequences, as does every promise that is broken), his betrayal cost him his kingdom. Having betrayed Clara and Esteban, the king promptly forgot everything Clara told him. By the time El Diablo returned, the king was busy studying a set of unicorn horns, and he dismissed the plotting fiend with a wave of his hand. Thus, he was not prepared when El Diablo launched his attack.

The creatures from the catacombs, released at last from their entrapment, relished their newfound freedom and overran the king's palace with devastating swiftness. The king was dethroned and put in a little red canoe. He was then taken to an island in the center of the black lake.

The children on the islands watched the entourage approach. The youthful king's eyes widened as he took in the oppressive darkness of his new home; his attempted plea for help became a strangled cry of despair.

The children on the lake were returned to their homes. Many, like Clara, had lived their final years in the dark cavern. But for the other children, their remaining years were full of love. They often talked about the girl who had made butterflies and roses and fairies out of sadness, and Clara's small acts of hope would go on to play a role in the lives of many.

But those are stories for another time.

On this last day, Death was waiting for Clara when she finally departed the Kingdom of Las Pozas and returned to Oaxaca City. The oppressive heat that had kept the city hostage for so long had finally abated; its heavy cloak lifted and was replaced by a cool breeze. The morning sky was unfurling in ribbons of pale pink and peach, cut through by the early rays of golden sun.

The day was just beginning, and nobody saw the old woman with a dragon on her shoulder walk out of the trunk of a gnarled tree, or the woman with the crown of roses waiting for her.

"Thank you," Clara said.

She had refused Catrina's gift when it was offered. However, knowing it was inevitable that she would meet Catrina again, Clara had asked for something else instead: an extra day, when the time came, to say goodbye.

Death and Clara found a seat on a bench facing the robin's-egg-blue house. It wasn't long before the door opened and Juana stepped out on her way to the mercado. A wave of profound love tore through Clara's chest, releasing the tears she had not allowed herself to shed in her role as magic maker for the children. A moment later, the door opened once more, and Esteban ran out. He called to Juana, who stopped and extended her hand. She smiled when Esteban caught up with her.

And then she looked up.

Clara rose from the bench, her bones creaking with age. Her eyes met Juana's.

"Clara?" The word was barely a whisper, but it found its target in Clara's heart.

In the moment that followed, there was only the rustling of a small breeze tangled in the leaves overhead. Juana's eyes brimmed with tears.

The next moment, she was running toward her daughter, with Esteban fast on her heels.

"¡Mi hija!" she cried, pulling Clara into an embrace. Esteban wrapped his arms around Clara's waist.

"What happened to you?" Juana finally asked, smoothing her hands over Clara's silver braids. Her fingers traced the lines of age on Clara's face. She held her daughter's frail hands, the skin papery and rough. Clara's fingertips were hard and scabbed.

"It's a long story," Clara replied. She smiled at Esteban.

"Come," Juana said, putting her arms protectively around Clara's shoulders. "You must tell us everything." She turned to Catrina. "Will you join us?"

Death shook her head. "Not today."

Juana led her daughter into their home. When the door opened, a whiff of chocolate drifted out, joining the swirls of scents wafting across Oaxaca City. Through the open door, Catrina spotted Clara's father dancing with a broom, keeping pace with the rapid beats of his favorite ranchera.

"Hola, Papi," Clara said.

The broom dropped from his hands as he reached for his daughter.

As evening fell over the city, the door to Clara's house opened. All that needed to be said had been said; embraces had been given. The two-headed dragon sat upon Esteban's shoulder, its small tail curled against Esteban's back, its scales picking up the light from a nearby lamppost. The black-and-white sun-and-moon pendant rested against Juana's chest.

Clara and her family approached the bench where Death awaited. Catrina rose to greet them.

"Thank you," Juana said to Catrina, knowing now the truth of the woman who had delivered Esteban to her care. Then she added, "Por favor cuídala."

Catrina nodded. "Always."

Clara released her mother's hand.

"I'm ready," she told Catrina, and she took the hand of Death.

Catrina snapped her fingers . . . and a new story began.

EPILOGUE

IN WHICH SOME INTERESTING DETAILS ARE REVEALED

WHAT IS MAGICAL REALISM?

Lotería portrays fantastical events occurring in an ordinary, real-world setting. This type of storytelling is called *magical realism*, and it is an important tradition in Latin American culture.

Writers of magical realism do not invent new worlds. Rather, we seek to reveal the magic that is hidden within our own world. In writing this story, I owe a huge debt of literary gratitude to some of the most influential and skilled writers of this genre, including Gabriel García Márquez, Isabel Allende, Jorge Luis Borges, and Laura Esquivel.

WHERE DID THE IDEAS ABOUT FREE WILL VERSUS DETERMINISM COME FROM?

The philosophical ideas explored in *Lotería* are not new; they have been debated by great minds throughout history. However, the conclusions at which I arrive are my own.

Free will generally refers to the ability to make choices voluntarily, the idea that one has control over one's actions. *Determinism* is a theory that states that all acts or occurrences are determined by preceding events.

In developing my thoughts on the issues of free will and determinism, I researched the work of many writers and philosophers, including:

Plato (c. 428–c. 348 BCE)

Aristotle (384–322 BCE)

St. Augustine (354–430)

St. Thomas Aquinas (1225–1274)

Thomas Hobbes (1588–1679)

René Descartes (1596–1650)

Gottfried Wilhelm Leibniz (1646–1716)

David Hume (1711–1776)

Immanuel Kant (1724–1804)

Arthur Schopenhauer (1788–1860)

Friedrich Nietzsche (1844–1900)

Ted Honderich (1933–)

Robert Kane (1938–)

Galen Strawson (1952–)

WHAT IS LA LOTERÍA?

La Lotería is a traditional Mexican game of chance, similar to bingo. It originated in Italy in the fifteenth century and was brought to Mexico in the late eighteenth century, when the country was a part of Spain.

In the game, each player chooses a board with a randomly created grid of sixteen pictures. In total there are fifty-four different images. The game is played using a deck of cards made up of all fifty-four images. A caller or singer (cantor) flips a card over to reveal the pictograph. In some variations of the game, the caller will sing (or call out) a riddle associated with each image, and players must guess the card. Players who have the image of that card on their board then place a marker (a chip or a black bean) on the appropriate picture.

There are many different versions of Lotería, and the players decide at the outset of the game which version they will play. In the most common form of the game, the first player to get four markers in a row (horizontal, vertical, or diagonal—or any other previously agreed-upon pattern) wins the game.

The fifty-four different images are Arrows, Barrel, Bell, Bird, Black One (Negrito), Bonnet, Boot, Bottle, Brave One, Canoe, Cello, Crown, Dandy (Catrín), Death, Deer, Devil, Drum, Drunkard, Fish, Flag,

Flowerpot, Frog, Hand, Harp, Heart, Heron, Ladder, Lady, Mandolin, Melon, Mermaid, Moon, Musician, Palm Tree, Parrot, Pear, Pine Tree, Prickly Pear Cactus, Raccoon, Rooster, Rose, Saucepan, Scorpion, Shrimp, Skull, Soldier, Spider, Star, Sun, Tree, Umbrella, Water Pitcher, Watermelon, and World. Each of these images is referenced at some point in this story.

WHAT IS DÍA DE LOS MUERTOS?

El Día de los Muertos (the Day of the Dead) is an important holiday in Mexico and other Latin American countries, honoring the lives of those who have passed away. To prepare for the celebration, families create altars in their homes or on their ancestors' graves, covering them with flowers, candles, photos, food, calaveras (candied skulls), and objects of special significance. The Day of the Dead celebrations unfold over two days, November 1 and 2, as families gather to symbolically awaken their ancestors and reconnect with their loved ones.

The representation of death as a lady named Catrina comes from *La Calavera Catrina,* an etching by José Guadalupe Posada from the early 1900s. It portrays a female skeleton wearing an elegant European hat. In the mid-1940s, the famous Mexican artist Diego Rivera painted a mural called *Dream of a Sunday Afternoon in the Alameda Central*, in which he depicted four hundred years of key historical figures. He included Posada's Calavera Catrina (though he added a body and a beautiful dress) as a way to represent the Mexican tradition of welcoming death and also the ancient Aztec reverence of Mictecacihuatl, goddess and ruler of the afterlife.

Rivera's depiction of Catrina has become the iconic image of death in Mexico, and it is quite common to see various representations of her, especially during the Día de los Muertos celebrations.

ARE THE PLACES IN *LOTERÍA* REAL?

Many of the places referred to in the book are real and have important historical significance.

OAXACA CITY

This is the capital of Oaxaca, a state in southern Mexico. In ancient times it was a cultural center of the Zapotec and Mixtec Indigenous populations. It is a World Heritage Site, a landmark city selected by the United Nations as having cultural and historical significance. The cathedral (Templo de Santo Domingo de Guzmán) and the Zócalo, the large public plaza, are both important locales in Oaxaca City, along with the many artisan and food markets.

LA GRUTA DE ORO

La Gruta de Oro is inspired by Las Grutas de Cacahuamilpa (also known by the local people as Salachi) in the Grutas de Cacahuamilpa National Park. *Cacahuamilpa* is a Nahuatl word meaning "peanut field."

Located in the state of Guerrero, Mexico, it is one of the largest cave systems in the world. For centuries, groundwater has filtered into it, promoting the growth of thousands of stalagmites and stalactites.

The cave system comprises ninety large "salons" (though only about a quarter of them have been explored). The average width of the salons is 130 feet, with a height ranging from 65 to 265 feet. Some of these salons are so large that they have been used to hold concerts and performances (one is even known as the Auditorium).

The pottery Esteban's brothers found would not have been out of place in Las Grutas de Cacahuamilpa. Excavations in the caverns have uncovered fragments of pottery dating back to pre-Hispanic times.

The massive formations they saw are also quite common in Las Grutas de Cacahuamilpa. Some well-known structures include the Organ (which looks like an organ-pipe cactus and makes the sound of an organ when knocked with a rock), the Fountain (a two-story structure that resembles a bubbling fountain), and the Bottle (a structure that looks like a towering soda bottle overflowing with foam).

EL ÁRBOL DEL TULE

This tree in Santa María del Tule, Oaxaca, is a true wonder and one of the largest of all living things (although not the tallest). According to some estimates, it is almost 50 feet in diameter, with a circumference of approximately 140 feet. The height is difficult to measure because of the tree's broad crown, but in 2005, laser measurements put it at about 120 feet. The tree is so vast that it was once believed to be multiple trees. DNA testing, however, proved that it is a single entity. Its scientific name is *Taxodium mucronatum* (Montezuma bald cypress), and its age is unknown, although annual growth rates suggest it is thousands of years old.

MONTE ALBÁN

Monte Albán is another World Heritage Site. This pre-Hispanic settlement was the ancient capital of the Zapotecs. At the height of its power, the city boasted close to thirty-five thousand inhabitants. It is an important archaeological site known for its architecture and the many astounding ancient artifacts recovered there, including a stunning collection of gold objects and jewelry.

ASREAN

The mythical land of Asrean is inspired by Aztlán, the legendary ancestral home of the Aztec people. *Aztecah* is a Nahuatl word, meaning "people from Aztlán."

THE KINGDOM OF LAS POZAS

The jungle world of Las Pozas is based on an actual surrealistic sculpture park of the same name in a subtropical rainforest in Xilitla, San Luis Potosí, Mexico. This mind-bending garden was created by Edward James, a British poet, and consists of more than eighty acres of land with twenty-seven buildings and sculptures. Dozens of trails wind around these towering structures, guiding visitors past natural and artificial pools and waterfalls. The park receives more than a hundred thousand visitors annually from all over the world, and the sculptures have been declared a national artistic monument.

Tenochtitlán, the ancient city upon which Mexico City was built, provided the inspiration for the king's lake with its floating islands. Tenochtitlán was the capital of the Aztec empire until it was captured by Spain in 1521. At its peak, Tenochtitlán was the largest city in pre-Columbian America.

The city was built on Lake Texcoco, a feat accomplished by creating a system of artificial islands, or chinampas. The man-made plots were built by weaving reeds into makeshift fences or borders that were anchored to the bottom of the lake. Then mud, sediment, and vegetation were piled up inside those borders until the top layer was visible over the surface of the water. Each plot of land could be used for any purpose (for example, to plant food or build a shelter).

Chinampas were separated by canals wide enough to allow for the passage of canoes. There were also raised causeways, beautiful floating gardens, and bridges that could be pulled away to isolate the city in the event of an attack.

WHAT WAS THE INSPIRATION FOR . . . ?

THE IMMORTAL KING

The scene in the king's tent and the king's quest for immortality were in part inspired by Oscar Wilde's *The Picture of Dorian Gray*, a story about a young man who makes a nefarious deal: trading his soul for eternal youth.

In Wilde's story, the passage of time is reflected in the portrait of Dorian Gray, which hangs on the wall and ages with each passing year—while the man himself remains forever young. It is a story about the pitfalls and unintended consequences of making ill-considered choices.

THE WHITE FAWN

The incident with the fawn that Clara encounters at the entrance to Las Pozas was inspired by an ancient Mayan myth. The story tells of a swift and elegant deer whose pale coloring made it easy prey for hunters. One day the deer was drinking water by a lake when it was surprised by a flurry of arrows shot by hunters intent on capturing it. The deer raced away, but it could not escape from the hunters. Just as an arrow was about to strike it, the deer fell into an underground cave.

The deer injured one of its legs in the fall, but it managed to survive. Its moans and groans alerted a group of genies who lived in the secret cave. They healed the deer with magic and allowed it to remain with them until it had completely recovered. The genies became fond of the small animal, and when the time came for the deer to depart, the genies granted it a wish. The deer asked for a way to keep itself safe from hunters, and the genies agreed. They covered the deer with dirt and asked the sun to change the color of the deer's fur. Little by little, the deer's fur darkened, until it had attained the same color as the dirt. The genies assured the deer that, with this gift, the hunters would no longer be able to see it. And they were right, or so the legend goes. Since that time, the deer has acquired almost mythical qualities: it is swift and seemingly capable of vanishing as soon as it's in the hunters' sights.

ESTEBAN'S TONGUE TWISTER

The tongue twister Clara teaches the parrot is a traditional Mexican trabalenguas. Another version of the tongue twister goes like this:

> *Tres tristes tigres tragaban trigo*
> *en tres tristes tastros en un trigal,*

En un trigal tres tristes tigres tragaban trigo
en tres tristes tastros.

(Three sad tigers gobbled up wheat
out of three sad pots in a wheat field,
In a wheat field three sad tigers gobbled
up wheat out of three sad pots.)

Another well-known tongue twister:

Erre con erre guitarra, erre con erre barril.
Mira que rápido ruedan, las ruedas del ferrocarril.

("R" with "R" guitar, "R" with "R" barrel.
Look at how quickly the wheels of the train roll.)

ACKNOWLEDGMENTS

This story unfolded very much like a game of *Lotería*. One moment led to another, which in turn was influenced by people and events entirely out of my control. I am grateful for all of it, and especially for the following people, whose auspicious arrival in this book's journey has played a significant role. In order of appearance:

My parents, who, of course, turned the first card (**Life**) and, in so doing, gave me Mexico, with all its myth and magic coursing through my veins.

Dave, Nico, Fía, and Santiago, who have rivaled Fate in shaping my destiny, and in whose hands I have placed mi **corazón**.

Gonzalo and Karin, who chose to host one of the best family-and-friends gatherings on record in Oaxaca City. **El gallo** kept us company through many a sunrise.

Rachel Atlan, Johnell DeWitt, Jami Gigot, Fiona Halliday, and Jess Townes, whose keen insights, observations, and turns of phrase are woven through these pages like ribbons in Clara's hair. Thank you for giving me a space in which to be **brave**.

Special thanks to Becky Shillington for showing me what I could not see (and for not allowing me to walk away). You are a **star**.

Ammi-Joan Paquette, without whose grace and guidance I would be lost. Like a **rose** in a magical garden, you always elicit a smile.

Katherine Harrison, whose editorial skills and knowledge are unmatched. The **crown** is yours.

Dana Sanmar, illustrator extraordinaire. I am humbled and honored that you chose my story to illuminate. You have been this story's **sun**.

Michelle Cunningham and Jen Valero, whose creativity and inspiration shine through in the gorgeous jacket and interior art. You are the story's **moon.**

Erin Clarke, Jake Eldred, Tracy Heydweiller, Melanie Nolan, and all the wonderful people involved in helping produce and edit this book. Your time, knowledge, and commitment to Clara's story have been a  gift. Special thanks to Artie Bennett, Alison Kolani, Jim Armstrong, Amy Schroeder, and Arely Guzmán for your attention to detail and care with words. Gianna Lakenauth has been lovely and essential every step of the way. Each of you has been critical to this story's ascent, a **ladder** without which *Lotería* would never have left the ground.

The entire marketing team, including Janine Perez, Caite Arocho, Laura Hernandez, Kristin Schulz, Emily DuVal, and Natalie Capogrossi, who took this book when it was just a seed and built a brilliant campaign for it that reaches for the sky. You are the **tree.**

Josh Redlich, whose role as publicist for this novel is not unlike that of a **musician,** making sure everyone hears the song of *Lotería.*

The entire sales team, with a shout-out to Brenda Conway, Dandy Conway, Stephanie Davey, Nic DuFort, Lauren Mackey, Deanna Meyerhoff, Carol Monteiro, Tim Mooney, Stacey Pyle, Amy Rockwell, Michele Sadler, and Kate Sullivan. I am profoundly moved to know that you have loved reading this story as much as I've loved writing it. I am so grateful that it is you who will be taking *Lotería* out into the **world.**

You, the reader, who has picked up this book and journeyed within it. I hope this story has inspired you or, at the very least, given you something to think about. I invite you to be like a **flowerpot,** nurturing your own ideas about these themes, pruning them, tending to them, and helping them grow into life adventures.

 And finally, **Death,** for she is always last. To her I make a small plea on behalf of the many loved ones in her care: *por favor cuídalos.*

READERS' GUIDE

1. Every choice Clara makes has a consequence, starting with her choice to open her window. Can you identify how her choices lead to the various events unfolding in her life? What do you think would have happened had she made different choices along the way?

2. How do you think Clara's story was influenced by the fact that the bird carried off the top card in the deck unseen? What role did Clara play in that event? How did her choice lead to a change in her destiny? How did it affect Life and Death's destiny? Was it a lucky choice after all?

3. How have your choices led to certain events? How do you think your choices have affected other people?

4. There are three key moments where Clara's fear or insecurity has big consequences for her: first, at the entrance to La Gruta de Oro; second, when the bird requests a drawing and she refuses; third, when she enters the tunnel under the wall of vines. How did each of these events change her story?

5. There is a moment when Clara thinks she's been betrayed: the scene with the rose. Was this actually a betrayal or a misunderstanding? How did this event help Clara? Can you think of a time in your life when you felt betrayed but everything turned out okay in the end? How might a misunderstanding lead us to make the wrong decision?

6. The scene with the spider is a turning point for Clara. She feels that she has hit her lowest moment and that all hope is lost. What keeps her going?

7. This is a story about free will, and throughout the book there are symbolic references to freedom. For instance, windows being opened, birds flying, oranges rolling away, words being trapped. Can you identify other ways in which freedom is represented? How are language and the choice of words being used to evoke feelings of freedom?

8. The lack of freedom is also explored throughout the story. Can you identify different ways that the characters are trapped? For instance, how do Clara's insecurities restrict her freedom? What role does grief play in trapping Esteban? How does our own view

of the world restrict us and limit our choices? How do the characters in the story free themselves from their various traps? What role do knowledge, courage, and hope play in their freedom?